THE ALIEN NEXT DOOR

4 BOOKS IN 1!

#1 THE NEW KID

#2 ALIENS FOR DINNER?!

#3 ALIEN SCOUT

#4 TRICK OR CHEAT?

by A. I. Newton
illustrated by Anjan Sarkar

little bee books

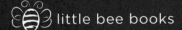 little bee books

An imprint of Bonnier Publishing USA
251 Park Avenue South, New York, NY 10010
Copyright © 2019 by Bonnier Publishing USA
All rights reserved, including the right of reproduction in whole or in part in any form.
Little Bee Books is a trademark of Bonnier Publishing USA, and associated colophon is a trademark of Bonnier Publishing USA.

Library of Congress Cataloging-in-Publication Data is available upon request.

Printed in the United States of America BVG 0219
ISBN 978-1-4998-0992-3

littlebeebooks.com
bonnierpublishingusa.com

THE ALIEN DOOR
NEXT

THE NEW KID

BY A. I. NEWTON   ILLUSTRATED BY ANJAN SARKAR

TABLE OF CONTENTS

1
THE NEW SCHOOL

THE NEW KID SAT ALONE IN the back of the bus. He was on his way to his first day at a new school.

Once again.

He watched as the other kids fooled around. They giggled and yelled. No one else seemed to be just sitting in their seat.

Except him. The new kid.

Once again.

Taking this "bus" thing to school with everyone else is really dumb, he thought. *Back home we got to school on our own. And much faster than in this clunky yellow hunk of metal. And instead of messing around the whole way like these kids, we had time to think and prepare for learning. But this . . .*

The new kid shook his head. No one on the bus seemed to even notice that he was there.

Here we go again, he thought. *Will anyone like me? Will I make any friends? Why do my parents have to move so much?*

The new boy sighed. He knew why they were always moving. They were research scientists. Their work took them from place to place. And every time they moved, he had to start over in a new school. He had to make new friends. He had to learn how things were done in a new place.

"Hey, Charlie!" one kid shouted at his friend. "Did you finish last week's homework?"

"I finished it this morning," another kid shouted back. "Right on time!"

The bus rocked with laughter.

The new kid didn't understand.

What was funny about waiting until the last minute to do your schoolwork? He didn't like always feeling different. He was tired of being the strange new kid once again.

And he missed his home.

I have friends back home. I know how stuff works there. All of this is so . . . different, so strange.

The bus slowed to a stop and the doors opened. The kids bounded down the stairs and ran toward the school.

The new kid got out of his seat. He walked slowly to the front of the bus to exit.

"Good luck today," said the bus driver. She smiled warmly at him. It made him feel a little better.

Here I go again, he thought. Then he took a deep breath, walked into the school, and hoped for the best.

2 THE NEW KID

HARRIS WALKER LOOKED around his second-grade classroom. He leaned over to his best friend, Roxy Martinez.

"I heard that a new boy is joining our class," said Harris. "He moved in next door to me yesterday."

"Really?" asked Roxy. "Where's he from?"

"Some place called Tragas," Harris replied. "I tried to look it up online. It's not even on a map!"

Their teacher, Ms. Graham, walked into the classroom.

"Good morning, class," she said. "We have a new student joining us today."

Harris whispered in Roxy's ear, "See, I told you!"

"Harris, is there a problem?" asked Ms. Graham.

"No, Ms. Graham," Harris said sheepishly.

"Well then, please pay attention. The new boy's name is Zeke. I want the entire class to make him feel welcome."

A whistling sound came from outside the classroom door.

Ms. Graham walked over and opened the door. A short boy with dark hair stood in the hall. Harris could see that he was wearing thick, black-rimmed glasses.

"You must be Zeke," said Ms. Graham.

"I am," replied the boy.

"Well, please come in," Ms. Graham said. "Why did you whistle at the door? Why didn't you just knock?"

Zeke looked confused. "Where I come from, that's how we ask permission to come into a room," he explained. Then he took a seat at an empty desk.

"Weird, huh?" Harris whispered to Roxy.

"I think it's kind of interesting," she whispered back.

Ms. Graham started writing on the board.

"Please write this homework assignment in your notebook or tablet," she said.

Ms. Graham, noticing Zeke, looked puzzled.

"Are you all right, Zeke?" she asked.

The new boy's eyes were shut tight. His fingertips were pressed against the sides of his head.

Zeke opened his eyes.

"Yes, Ms. Graham. I'm fine," he said. "I was just writing down the assignment."

Zeke held up his tablet. The assignment was there, all typed out.

"How did he do that?" Harris whispered to Roxy.

"Maybe he has a wireless keyboard under his desk," Roxy replied.

"But his hands were—"

"Harris, do you have a question?" asked Ms. Graham.

"No, Ms. Graham," he said, looking down.

At lunch that day, Harris and Roxy sat together as usual. Zeke sat by himself.

"I feel bad for Zeke," said Roxy. "He doesn't know anyone. I'm going to ask him to sit with us."

"Why?" Harris asked. "We don't even know him!"

"But he's your neighbor, and this is our chance to get to know him," Roxy replied. Then she called out to Zeke, "Zeke, why don't you come eat lunch with us?"

Zeke picked up a round metal ball with blinking lights he had on the table in front of him and joined Harris and Roxy where they were sitting.

"What's that?" Harris asked.

"My lunch container," Zeke explained.

"Odd-looking lunch box," Harris mumbled.

"So how do you like Jefferson Elementary School so far?" Roxy asked.

"It is . . . different," said Zeke.

Zeke opened his blinking metal lunch box and pulled out a large green ball. Pink strings dangled from the ball. He shoved the whole thing into his mouth. His cheeks puffed out. He looked like he was eating two softballs at the same time.

Without moving his mouth at all, Zeke's cheeks slowly got smaller and smaller.

"What are you eating?" asked Harris.

"It's called a dweelop," Zeke explained. "It's a fruit that grows all over Tragas, where I come from."

"But you didn't even chew it," Harris said.

"It's pretty soft," Zeke replied.

A few minutes later, the bell sounded. Lunchtime was over. Harris cleared his tray and headed back to class.

This new kid is definitely weird! he thought.

3
ZEKE AT HOME

AFTER SCHOOL WAS OVER,
Zeke walked back to his new house,
opening the front door. He had just
finished his first day at a new school.
He was happy to be home.

"How was your first day,
Zekelabraxis?" asked a voice from
across the living room.

Zeke looked over and saw a creature with green skin. It had five eyes, and six tentacles extending from its shoulders.

"Xad! I thought we were going to use Earth names and bodies. . . ." Zeke whined.

"You are indeed correct, Zeke," said Xad.

The green being began to glow. When the glowing stopped, a human-looking man stood in its place. He was short with black hair. He wore the same thick, black-rimmed glasses that Zeke wore.

Zeke's mom joined them.

"Brezkat plitnob, Zekelabraxis?" she said. She floated into the room, two feet off the ground. She, too, had green skin, and she had seven eyes and four tentacles.

"Quar!" Zeke said to his mom. "English only while we are here, remember?" said Zeke.

Zeke's mom nodded. She glowed and took her human form. She was tall and thin, with shoulder-length hair.

"Here, Quar, you forgot your translation glasses," said Zeke's dad. He handed his wife a pair of thick, black-rimmed glasses. She slipped them on.

Zeke thought about the translation glasses. And how, by smoothly translating the language of Tragas into the language of whatever planet they were on, they allowed his parents to do their research and allowed him to go to school.

"So, how was your first day, Zeke?" Quar repeated her question. This time, it was translated into English.

"They have very strange customs on this planet," said Zeke. "It is not like Tragas. They don't absorb their food through their cheeks. They chew it with something called 'teeth.' And they can't mind-project to write."

"Speaking of writing," said Zeke's mom, "do you have any missions from school?"

"On Earth they call it 'homework,'" Zeke explained. "And yes, I do."

Zeke read the assignment on his tablet. Then he pressed a button on the table next to him. A large screen appeared just above his head.

Zeke pressed his fingertips against the sides of his head. He shut his eyes tightly and thought about the answers to his homework questions. Numbers appeared on the giant screen.

To Zeke, he was just doing his homework—the same way he did it on his home planet of Tragas.

$$49 + 82 = 131$$
$$6 \times 12 =$$

ALIENS!

THAT SAME DAY AFTER
school, Harris sat at the desk in
his room. He was trying to do his
homework. But all he could think
about was the strange new kid in his
class. He decided to call Roxy.

"What did you think of that new
kid, Zeke?" Harris asked when Roxy
picked up the phone.

"He was nice," she replied.

"He was weird," said Harris.

"Just because someone is different doesn't mean they're weird," Roxy pointed out.

Harris thought about that for a moment. He wasn't sure what to think of Zeke.

"I know, but still, I think there's something off about him. Anyway, I have to finish my homework," Harris said. "See ya tomorrow."

When his homework was done, Harris opened the latest issue of his favorite comic book, *Tales from Alien Worlds!* He flopped onto his bed and opened it. He saw alien spaceships zooming through the air. They passed tall orange towers that glowed.

What a cool alien world this is! Harris thought.

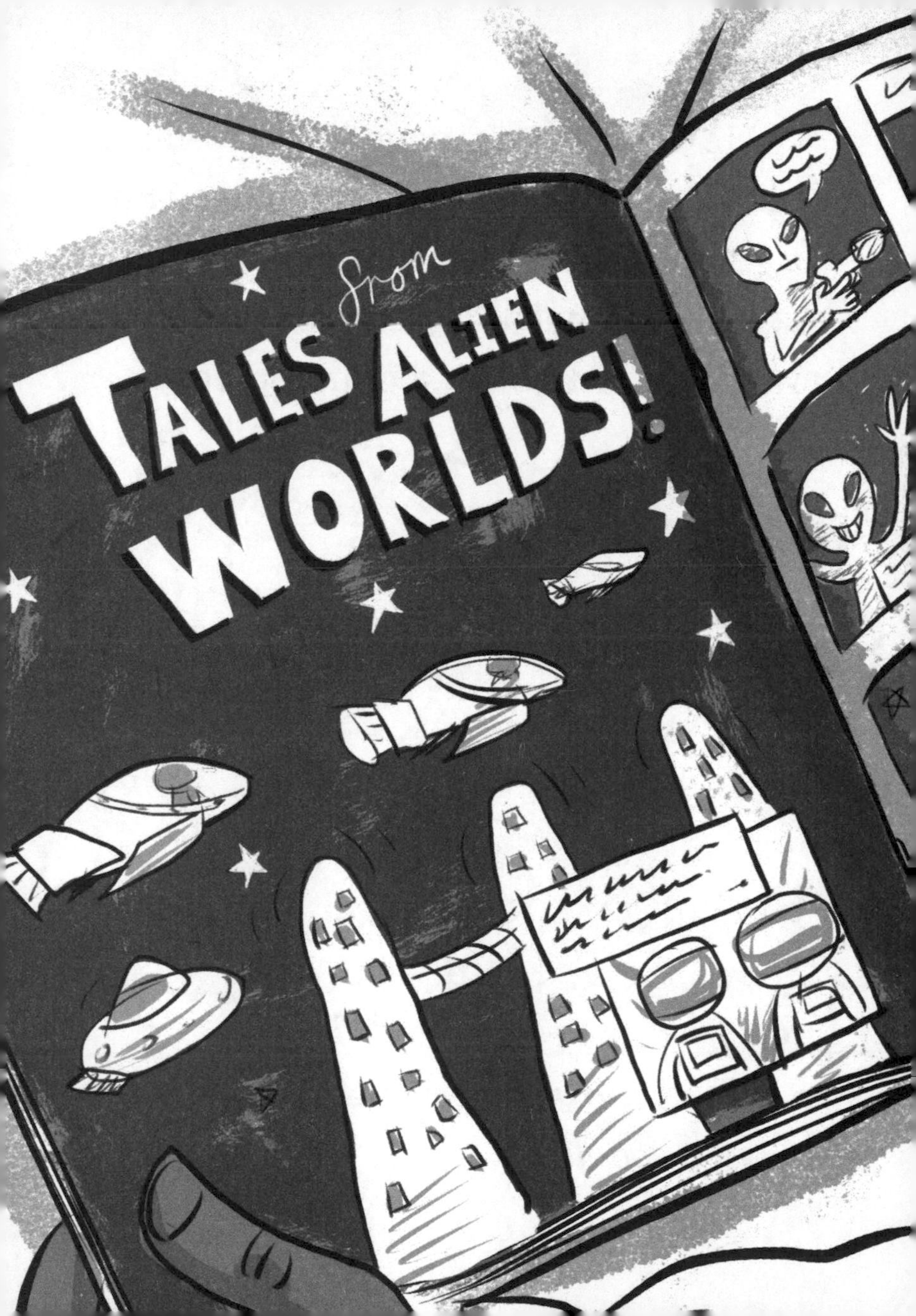

TALES from ALIEN WORLDS!

He flipped the page. There was a picture of an alien with his eyes shut tight. The alien's fingertips pressed against his head. In front of the alien, words appeared on a giant screen.

That's how Zeke wrote on his tablet! This is too weird.

Harris finished the comic. He looked out the window at Zeke's house. *Why is it always dark over there?*

He got ready for bed, but couldn't stop thinking about Zeke.

The next day at school, Harris found Roxy at recess. She had a soccer ball at her feet. Roxy and Harris were both on the Jefferson Elementary School soccer team.

"Let's practice," she said.

Roxy kicked the ball across the playground. Harris chased it down and kicked it back.

Roxy looked and saw Zeke balanced on a swing on just one finger. His body stood upside down, straight as an arrow. She and Harris ran over to him.

"What the heck are you doing?" Harris asked.

Zeke looked at them.

Roxy's next kick rolled right past Harris. Instead of paying attention to the ball, he was staring at the swing set.

"Do you see that?" Harris asked, pointing.

I can't tell them the truth, Zeke thought. *That this exercise helps me mind-project more clearly.*

"I am planning on trying out for the gymnastics team," Zeke said. "I was good at gymnastics in Tragas."

Harris had his doubts. But before he could say anything else, the bell rang. Recess was over. Harris and Roxy hurried back into the school.

That evening after dinner, Harris joined his dad in front of the TV. It was time for the Monster Movie of the Week. Harris and his dad never missed it.

"This should be a good one," said Harris's dad. "It's called *Monster Aliens from Planet Z.*"

The movie began. A giant alien spaceship landed right in the middle of a park. People ran in panic.

The spaceship's door slid open. An alien walked out. Only, the alien didn't walk on its feet. It walked upside down on its fingertips.

Just like Zeke! Harris thought. *That's it! That explains everything. My new neighbor is definitely an alien!*

THE NEXT DAY AT SCHOOL,

Zeke felt bored.

Well, that didn't take long, he thought.
*I always get so worried about starting a
new school, but in this place, everything
they do is so simple. If I can't be home,
I wish I were back on Charbock.*

Charbock was the last planet Zeke's family had researched.

At least there, kids could do cool stuff like teleport from place to place. And control the weather with their minds. It was a very interesting planet. Not like Earth, Zeke thought as he entered the science lab.

"Okay, class, today's experiment is all about colors," said Mr. Mills, the science teacher. "We are going to combine certain colors to create other colors. In front of you are red, green, yellow, and blue solutions. Experiment and see how combining the colors changes them into new ones."

Zeke combined yellow and blue to make green. He combined blue and red to make purple. Then he mixed red and yellow to make orange. He was the first one in the class to finish.

Zeke glanced over at Harris and Roxy. They were still combining colors, but Harris was also staring at him.

Why does Harris keep staring at me like that? Zeke wondered. *Could he actually suspect that I'm not from this planet?*

As the other kids worked with the basic colors, Zeke got an idea.

This could be fun, he thought.

He combined all the solutions in one glass beaker. Then he grabbed the beaker with both hands. He sent vibrations from his hands into the glass and the colors inside the beaker started to swirl.

A few seconds later, Zeke had created a twirling rainbow right inside his beaker.

He glanced toward Roxy and Harris.

Roxy saw the rainbow and smiled. "Wow, that is *so* cool!"

But Harris's eyes opened wide.

"How did you do that, Zeke?" asked Harris. "That's impossible!"

"What's impossible?" asked Mr. Mills. He walked over to Zeke's table and saw the rainbow spinning in his beaker.

"Actually, Harris, it is not impossible," said Mr. Mills. "There is a chemical you can add to your colors that will make that happen."

Harris frowned. Then Mr. Mills turned to Zeke.

"However, Zeke, that chemical is kept in a drawer labeled DO NOT OPEN." Mr. Mills explained. "I admire your curiosity and inventiveness. But please do not open any drawers without permission, there are some dangerous things in there."

Zeke couldn't admit that he didn't use any chemicals, he just used his powers. He stayed quiet. His parents were very clear about revealing his powers to anyone on Earth.

"Unlike Charbock, Earth has not yet made contact with anyone outside of Earth," his father had said on their journey to their new planet. "You must never reveal your powers to anyone there."

The bell rang ending science lab.

As he left the room, Harris looked at Zeke and shook his head.

What if he finds out I'm an alien?
Zeke thought. *I could ruin my parents'
entire mission here.*

Zeke walked from the lab. *This
is going to be a long school year,* he
thought.

6 MOM AND DAD

AFTER SCHOOL, HARRIS AND Roxy walked home together.

"You know, I don't think you've been very welcoming to Zeke," said Roxy. "Just because he's different from you doesn't mean he isn't nice."

"I still think he's strange," Harris said.

"Well, I like him," said Roxy. "Is
that why you *don't* like him? I can be
friends with both of you, you know."

"That's not it," said Harris. "I've
just seen him do some crazy stuff."

"And all of what you call 'crazy stuff' has a logical explanation," said Roxy. "I just think you're looking for reasons to not like Zeke."

Roxy turned onto her block. Harris kept walking.

He thought about what Roxy had said. Then he shrugged it off.

That evening at dinner, Harris's parents asked him about Zeke.

"How is that new boy doing?" asked his mom.

"I hope you are trying to make friends with him," added his dad.

"I don't know," said Harris. "He does all kinds of strange stuff. He even balanced on his fingertips, like the aliens in that movie, Dad."

"Harris, come on," said his dad. "You're too old to not know the difference between movies and real life."

"No, Dad, it's real!" Harris insisted. "I'm telling you the truth."

"Remember how much trouble you had making friends when you started at Jefferson until you met Roxy?" asked his mom. "I would hope that you would be extra nice to new kids who are trying to fit in."

"But, Mom, I—"

"I'm sure that if you take the time to get to know Zeke, you'll discover that he's just a normal kid like you," Mom said. "He might be different, but that's no reason not to be his friend."

Harris went to his room after dinner and started his homework. But again he had trouble concentrating.

Everyone is telling me that I'm wrong, but I know I'm not. I'm going to prove, once and for all, that Zeke is an alien!

7

OPERATION ALIEN REVEAL

THE NEXT DAY AT LUNCH,
Harris put his plan into motion. As
he and Roxy walked into the cafeteria,
Harris spotted Zeke.

"Hey, Zeke, why don't you sit with
us for lunch?" he called out.

"Well, I'm glad you finally decided
to be nice to him," said Roxy, smiling.

The three sat together at a table. Roxy pulled out a tunafish sandwich. Harris bit into his PB&J. Zeke took out a long purple string. He put one end into his mouth and slurped up the entire thing. Then he pulled out another one.

"What's that?" Harris asked in a very friendly voice.

"Gardash strands," said Zeke. "They are very popular in Tragas."

"Speaking of Tragas, where exactly is it?" Harris asked.

"South of here," replied Zeke.

"On this continent?" Harris asked.

"No," said Zeke, slurping down another gardash strand.

"So what's it next to?" asked Harris.

"Quarzinta," replied Zeke.

"I never heard of that either," said Harris.

"Someone doesn't know his geography," Zeke said.

Roxy giggled, and Harris looked down, embarrassed. His plan was going nowhere.

"So what's it like in Tragas?" asked Roxy.

"Well, there is bright yellow water in the lakes," said Zeke. "We have elevators that travel sideways, not up and down. And the snow is a glowing blue."

If that doesn't sound like an alien planet, I don't know what does! Harris thought.

"Sounds wonderful!" said Roxy. "So, I had an idea. Maybe we should all hang out this weekend. How about Saturday?"

Harris's eyes opened wide.

Hang out? he thought. *With an alien? That's too weird. But if I say no, Roxy will think I'm being mean.*

"I would like that, thank you," said Zeke.

"Why don't we all go to your house, Harris?" asked Roxy. "You have the biggest TV and some cool games. And wait till you meet his parents, Zeke. They're so nice!"

"Um . . . sure," said Harris. What else could he say?

Harris felt trapped.

Today is Thursday, he thought. *That only gives me one more day to prove that Zeke is an alien before I have to hang out with him—in my own house!*

8

MISSION: EARTH

THAT EVENING AT HOME, Zeke talked to his parents.

"I like some of the Earth stuff at school," he explained. "The bell that sounds between classes is the same tone as my meditation chime back on Tragas. It helps my mind-projection."

"Well that sounds nice," said Quar.

"I don't really like taking the school bus," said Zeke. "But the way the folding door opens is very clever."

"Have you met any nice Earth kids?" asked Xad.

"I think I have made a new friend," said Zeke. "Her name is Roxy. She has been very nice to me."

"That's wonderful, Zeke," said Quar.

"Oh, and Roxy and I have been invited to visit the home of the boy who lives next door, Harris, this weekend," said Zeke. "I'm a little worried about him. I think he may suspect that I'm what they would call an 'alien.'"

"I know you miss it, Zeke," said Quar.

"It *is* the official sport of Tragas," Zeke said. "And no one on Earth has even heard of it!"

"Well, I have some good news for you," said Xad. "I've been adapting our long-range communications device to pick up broadcasts of Bonkas matches from Tragas. Maybe that will help you feel less homesick."

"Be careful, Zeke," said Xad. "You remember what I told you about Earth."

"I know," said Zeke. "I'm trying to fit in."

"Sounds to me like you're doing okay, Zeke," said Quar.

"But I still miss my friends on Tragas," said Zeke. "And it's Bonkas season there already. I'm going to have to miss another season watching my favorite team play."

"Thanks, Xad!" said Zeke. "So, how long are you planning on staying on Earth?"

"It's hard to say, Zeke," said Xad. "It depends upon what my bosses want to learn about humans. Right now, we're assigned to study human clothing. Why do humans dress the way they do?"

"Why do boys and girls often dress so differently?" Quar continued. "Why do humans wear different clothing for work, play, fancy parties, and other things?"

A video appeared on the giant overhead screen where Zeke did his homework.

"This was our research at the giant group of stores today," said Xad.

"On Earth, they call this a 'mall,'" said Zeke.

The video showed a family with three children. Each kid held a different color shirt. They passed the shirts back and forth in front of a mirror.

"This one doesn't match my eyes," said one kid.

"This is the wrong color for my hair!" said another.

Zeke and his parents laughed. On Tragas, everyone wore the same style of clothing.

"Earth people can be pretty silly," said Zeke. "I can see why you'd want to study them."

IT WAS ALREADY FRIDAY, and Harris was worried. Zeke would be coming to hang out at Harris's house the next day unless he was able to prove Zeke was an alien.

At recess, several grades were out on the playground together.

"I've got the soccer ball, Harris," said Roxy. "Ready?"

Roxy kicked the ball to him. Then she noticed Zeke standing all by himself.

"Hey, Zeke, do you want to play soccer with us?" she called out.

Zeke trotted over to Roxy.

"I don't know how to play soccer," he said.

"It's easy," Roxy said. "You kick the ball to another player or into the goal. And you can't touch the ball with your hands. Try it."

Zeke ran toward Harris.

"Harris, kick the ball to Zeke!" she shouted.

Harris kicked the ball right at Zeke.

Zeke stopped and got ready to kick it back. But when the ball reached him, it skipped over his foot.

To his amazement, Harris watched as Zeke just stood still and lifted one hand into the air. Zeke wiggled his hand. The soccer ball slowed down, stopped, then started rolling back toward Zeke.

Harris immediately turned to Roxy.

Did she just see that? Harris wondered. *That's proof that Zeke is an alien!*

But Roxy's back was to both boys just then. She had turned to talk to her friend, Samantha.

I can't believe that Roxy didn't see that, thought Harris. *I'm never going to prove this before tomorrow.*

Harris looked down and saw the ball speeding toward him. He kicked it to Zeke.

Again, Zeke missed the ball. It rolled toward the far corner of the playground. This time, Zeke chased after it.

When Zeke reached the ball, he saw a kindergartener crying under a basketball hoop.

"What's the matter?" asked Zeke, walking over to him.

The little boy pointed up at the hoop.

"My balloon slipped out of my hand and now it's stuck up there!" sobbed the boy.

Zeke looked up and saw the balloon stuck against the rim.

"I can get that for you," he said.

I'll bet you can, thought Harris. *You're probably going to fly up to the hoop, or transport the balloon down or something. You're going to do something weird, I know it! And this time, Roxy has to see it.*

"Roxy, look!" Harris called out. He pointed at Zeke.

This is it! Harris thought. *Roxy is finally going to see Zeke do something that will prove he's an alien!*

But when Roxy turned around, all she saw was a tall sixth grader from the basketball team leap up and grab the balloon's string. He handed it to the kindergartener.

Roxy rolled her eyes at Harris and shook her head.

Harris sighed. *I guess an alien is coming to my house after all!*

10 NEW FRIENDS

HARRIS WOKE UP SATURDAY

morning and was very nervous. Zeke was coming to his house today.

Around noon, both Roxy and Zeke arrived.

"Hi, Roxy, so nice to see you," said Harris's mom.

"Thanks for having us over, Mrs. Walker," said Roxy. "This is our new friend, Zeke."

"Welcome, Zeke," said Mrs. Walker.

"We've heard a whole lot about you from Harris," said Harris's dad.

"Thank you, Mr. Walker, Mrs. Walker," said Zeke. "I'm glad to be here."

"So," said Harris, "who wants to play some video games?"

Roxy raised her hand. Zeke looked at her and raised his as well.

The three friends sat down in front of the TV and each picked up a controller.

"This one is called *Cosmic Comet Blast*," said Harris. "The idea is to blast comets out of the sky before they crash into Earth. Ready . . . go!"

On the big screen, giant comets streaked across the sky.

"Fire your laser cannons!" shouted Harris.

Harris blasted a few comets. Roxy blew up a few more. Zeke wasn't doing much at first, but soon he destroyed every comet he aimed at.

"That was amazing, Zeke!" said Roxy.

"Yeah," said Harris. "Are you sure you never played this game before?"

"I'm sure, Harris," said Zeke. "They don't have video games in Tragas."

"No video games!" Harris said. "What do you do for fun?"

"We race in our zumda cycles," said Zeke. "We play Bonkas, which uses thin sticks and ten Bonkas balls. And we make up project-o-stories on our holo-screens."

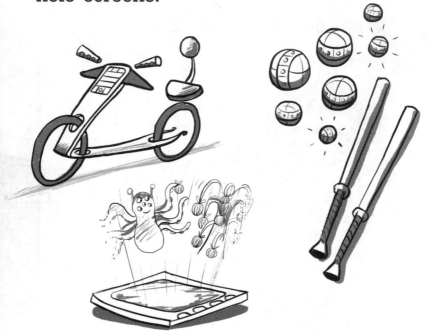

"How come I've never heard of any of that stuff?" asked Harris skeptically.

"Oh, well, Tragas is very far away," explained Zeke.

"Who wants pizza?" Harris's mom called from the kitchen.

"What is pizza?" asked Zeke.

"Come on," said Harris. "You don't have pizza on Tragas? I thought everyone ate pizza." *That's definitely proof he's an alien!* thought Harris.

"I'm happy to try it," said Zeke.

Zeke, Roxy, Harris, and his parents sat around the kitchen table. They each grabbed a slice of pizza.

"I have never tasted anything like this," said Zeke. "I like it."

"Zeke, what do your parents do?" asked Mr. Walker.

"They are researchers," Zeke explained. "They move from place to place. That's why I move around so much. That's why I'm always starting over in a new school."

"That must be hard," said Mrs. Walker.

"I get used to it, I guess," Zeke said. "It helps when I make new friends." He smiled at Harris and Roxy.

"I know what I wanted to tell you, Zeke," said Roxy. "I'm trying out for the school play."

"Don't tell me that they don't have plays in Tragas," Harris said.

Zeke laughed. "No, we have plays in Tragas. In fact, I like to act. I have been in a few plays."

"Maybe you should try out, Zeke," said Roxy. "It's a great way to meet new kids."

"Thanks," said Zeke. "Maybe I will."

After lunch, the kids watched a movie—*Zombie Invasion from Beneath the Earth!*

"You have movies in Tragas, right?" asked Harris.

"Yes," replied Zeke. *Except ours are 4-D holo-projections. But I have to be careful what I tell Harris!* he thought to himself.

When the movie ended, it was time for Roxy and Zeke to go home.

"Thank you," said Zeke as he headed for the door. "I had a nice time."

"See you Monday," said Roxy.

"Well, Zeke seems like a very nice boy, Harris," said Mrs. Walker when Zeke and Roxy had gone. "All you had to do was give him a chance."

"I did have fun with Zeke today," Harris admitted.

But I still think he's an alien, Harris thought. *And one of these days I'm going to prove it!*

Zeke walked back over to his home next door.

"How was your visit, Zeke?" asked Xad.

"I had fun," Zeke said. "I think things might be okay here on Earth. I'm off to a good start. After all, I have already made two new friends!"

THE ALIEN

NEXT DOOR

ALIENS FOR DINNER?!

BY A. I. NEWTON

ILLUSTRATED BY ANJAN SARKAR

2

TABLE OF CONTENTS

THE INVITATION

HARRIS WALKER RAN OUT onto the Jefferson Elementary School soccer field. It was Friday afternoon, and practice was about to begin.

Harris's best friend, Roxy Martinez, trotted up next to him.

"It was fun having Zeke over last weekend, right? I hope you're done with that 'Zeke is an alien' nonsense," she said.

Zeke was Harris's new next-door neighbor. He had only been at their school for a couple of weeks.

But Harris believed that Zeke was an alien—a real-life alien who somehow came here from another planet. Harris saw Zeke do things that would be impossible for any human kid to do, like move things with his mind, make rainbows suddenly appear in the science lab, and even balance on his fingertips.

"I did have fun. Zeke's a nice kid," Harris replied.

But I still think he's an alien, Harris thought.

Coach Ruffins blew his whistle.

"Okay, everyone, let's get this practice going!" he shouted.

Harris, Roxy, and rest of the players spent the next hour working on passing, shooting, and defense.

When the practice was nearly over, Harris saw Zeke walking onto the field. A soccer ball flew right toward the front of Zeke's head.

"Look out!" Harris shouted.

He watched in amazement as the ball changed direction, all by itself. It swung around Zeke's head and continued into the goal.

Harris turned to Roxy.

"Did you see that?!" he asked her, sure that she must have seen Zeke control the ball with his mind.

"Yeah," said Roxy, "the ball came so close to hitting Zeke's head! I'm glad he didn't get hurt."

Drats! Harris thought. *From her angle, it must have looked normal.*

"What's up, Zeke?" Harris asked casually as the three friends walked back toward the school.

"I just wanted to thank you again for a great time hanging out at your house, Harris," said Zeke. "And also to invite the both of you to my house tomorrow. We could hang out and play. And my parents are anxious to meet you."

"Sounds great!" said Roxy. She looked at Harris, waiting for him to accept, too.

This is the perfect opportunity to research Zeke's alien family, Harris thought. *I can finally find out what's behind those dark curtains and prove once and for all that he's an alien!*

"I'd love to come over, Zeke," Harris said, giving Roxy a look that said: *See? I don't think he's an alien anymore.*

"Great!" said Zeke. "See you tomorrow!"

ZEKE BURST THROUGH the front door of his house. "Xad! Quar! I have something to tell you," he shouted.

"I'm up here, Zeke," said his father, Xad.

Zeke looked up and saw his dad floating near the ceiling. He sat in a cross-legged position. A metal helmet rested on his head.

Xad then drifted down, landing on the floor.

"I was just mind-transferring some of my latest research," Xad explained. "Did you know that humans wear different shoes in the rain and snow than they do on a sunny day?"

"I guess they don't have *adap-a-fiber* here," said Zeke.

"What is it, Zeke?" Quar, his mother, called out. She appeared in a shimmering haze to them, holo-projecting her image. "I'm out in the garden."

"Harris and Roxy have agreed to come here tomorrow," Zeke said.

"That's great, Zeke," said Quar. "We are so glad that you made two new friends so quickly."

"Yes, and it will also be the perfect chance to do some research on humans—up close!" said Xad.

"Don't forget you have to be as 'human' as possible, too," said Zeke, crossing his arms. "I don't want my friends to wonder what you're doing."

"Don't worry, Zeke," said Quar. "We will be careful and respectful."

Zeke nodded, then settled down to mind-project his homework.

At the same time, next door in Harris's house, Harris told his parents about Zeke's invitation.

"That's wonderful!" said Harris's mom.

"Well, I'm just glad you've given up on that crazy alien stuff," said his dad.

Harris nodded to reassure his parents, but thought: *Tomorrow, I'm finally going to prove that Zeke really is an alien!*

3 ZEKE'S HOUSE

THE NEXT DAY, HARRIS AND
Roxy arrived at Zeke's house.

"Can I take your coats?" Zeke asked
them.

Harris looked around the front

hallway. He was surprised at how normal everything looked, almost like his own house. But when he started to slip off his coat, he felt someone take it from him. Zeke and Roxy were standing right in front of him.

So who took my coat?

Turning around, Harris saw a pair of mechanical hands extending from the wall. They grabbed his coat, then Roxy's, and pulled them into an open panel in the wall.

"What was that?" Harris asked.

"Cool! So high-tech!" said Roxy.

Before Zeke could respond, Xad and Quar joined them.

"Roxy, Harris, I'd like you to meet my Quar and Xad," said Zeke. "I mean . . . my mom and dad."

"It's a pleasure," said Quar. "You both have been very kind to Zeke."

Zeke noticed that Xad was staring at Roxy's sneakers. They were bright blue with orange laces.

He leaned in and whispered. "Xad, try to not be so obvious about studying my friends' clothes!"

"Why don't we have some lunch?" suggested Quar.

Everyone gathered at the kitchen table. The table had no legs. It was just a clear disk hanging in midair.

How does that work? wondered Harris. *This must be alien technology, too! How is Roxy not bothered by this?*

"So, Harris, Roxy, what do you like to eat?" asked Xad.

"Burgers and hot dogs!" replied Harris.

"I like sandwiches and burritos," said Roxy.

Xad and Quar looked at each other, worried. They mind-projected their thoughts to each other so no one else could hear them.

Can our food replicator create these Earth dishes? Xad thought.

I don't know. It is only set to create Tragas food, Quar replied.

Zeke overheard this conversation in his mind. He jumped up from the table.

"I'll take care of lunch!" he said.

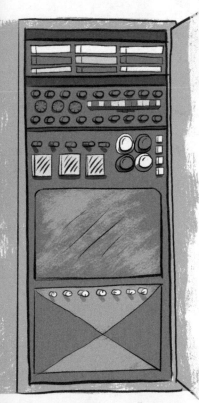

Zeke walked over to what looked like a huge floor-to-ceiling refrigerator. He pulled open the door. What only Zeke could see was that behind the door was actually a panel of switches, buttons, and blinking lights—the Tragas Food Replicator 3000.

The Tragas Food Replicator 3000 can create any food you ask it to . . . as long as it's served on Tragas! Zeke thought. *I hope it can make something close to these Earth foods!* He began pushing buttons and entering commands.

Harris leaned over to see what Zeke was doing, but Roxy poked him in the shoulder.

"Don't be rude!" she whispered. "What someone else keeps in their fridge is *their* business!"

A few minutes later, Zeke returned to the table with his arms full.

Harris stared at the steaming plates of food. *How did Zeke heat those up in the fridge?* he thought.

"Why does the burrito have purple polka dots?" he asked. "And how come the hot dog is a big circle?"

"These are the Tragas versions of those foods," Xad said quickly.

Harris bit into his hot dog and was surprised. It tasted sweet, like a candy bar.

Roxy tasted her burrito. She looked at Harris, and her face scrunched up. He could tell that her burrito must have tasted as weird as his hot dog.

Roxy smiled at Zeke. "Well, it sure is different. But good!" she said.

When everyone finished lunch, Zeke stood up.

"Why don't we go to my room and play some games?" he suggested.

The three friends headed to Zeke's room.

I can't wait to see what kind of alien stuff he has in there! thought Harris.

4

PLAYTIME!

THE THREE FRIENDS stepped into Zeke's room. *Wow, it looks similar to my room*, Harris thought. They all sat down on a couch.

"Want to play a game?" Zeke asked.

He pressed a button under the couch, and a large screen blazed to life on the ceiling. The three of them looked up at the screen, and Harris's jaw dropped.

"I thought you didn't have video games in Tragas," said Harris.

"Well, not like the ones we played at your house," Zeke said.

"I've never seen a screen like that!" Roxy said.

That's because it's alien technology! Harris thought.

"We have a lot of high-tech stuff in Tragas. This game is called *Monster Mania*. You battle all kinds of monsters. But here's the coolest part."

Instead of giving Harris and Roxy hand-held controllers, Zeke placed a helmet onto each of their heads, and then placed one on himself.

"You create and control your avatar onscreen with your mind, not your fingers!" said Zeke. "And the monsters you battle also come from your own mind."

Zeke's avatar was a giant bird. When a fire-breathing, three-headed dragon appeared, Zeke controlled his bird with his mind and defeated the dragon.

Roxy's avatar was a warrior with a sword, shield, and armor. She battled a T. rex, but the dinosaur quickly clobbered her.

"This is hard!" she said.

"Keep playing. You'll get the hang of it," said Zeke.

Harris's avatar was a superhero with bulging muscles and a long cape. He fought a cyclops who swung a big wooden club. Despite his superpowers, Harris's avatar was overcome.

An army of trolls soon rushed at the three avatars.

"Work together!" said Zeke. "If we focus our thoughts on each others' avatars, we can defeat these trolls as a team!"

Harris concentrated really hard. After a few seconds, his avatar began fighting alongside the others, and they soon defeated the trolls.

"Cool game, Zeke!" Harris said. He was so caught up in the fun that he had stopped thinking that this game—like Zeke—might be from another planet.

"How about a movie?" asked Zeke.

"Sure," said Roxy, removing her game helmet.

Zeke pressed another button. The screen spun around and around. When it stopped spinning, a movie started.

"*Danger in the Deep*!" said Zeke. "It's one of my favorites. And it's a 4-D holo-projection! You feel like you're in the movie."

"Let me guess," Harris said. "High-tech stuff from Tragas?"

"Yup," said Zeke, smiling, and then they settled in for the movie.

Harris suddenly felt himself surrounded by yellow water. A giant sea creature with twelve tentacles swam past him.

"Wow!" he said. "I feel like I'm at the bottom of the ocean!"

"I hope that sea monster doesn't bite me!" Roxy said.

When the movie ended, the three friends headed downstairs. It was time to go home. Zeke's parents met them in the hallway.

"Thanks for having us over," said Roxy.

But Xad didn't seem to hear her and instead pointed at the label on Harris's T-shirt.

"What is the purpose of this?" Xad asked.

That's really strange, Harris thought. *Who doesn't know what a shirt label is?*

"Um, it tells you the size and fabric, and how to clean it," Harris explained.

"Fascinating," said Xad, making notes on a tablet.

A panel in the hallway wall slid open. Out popped Harris's and Roxy's jackets.

"Thanks again!" said Roxy.

"Bye, Zeke!" said Harris as they headed out the door and walked back to Harris's house.

"What a cool house and family! He's a really nice kid, isn't he?" said Roxy. She got on her bike and rode away.

Harris couldn't believe she didn't comment on everything weird that happened there. *Yeah, it was fun, but based on the way-too-advanced tech, the crazy food, and Zeke's strange parents, he's definitely a nice* **alien** *kid!*

5
MOMS AND DADS

ZEKE JOINED HIS PARENTS in the living room. All three floated upside down in the air, up near the ceiling.

"I'm not certain it was wise to show your friends all that Tragas technology," said Xad.

"*You're* the one who was so obvious when you inspected their clothes!" Quar said.

"I think it's all okay," said Zeke. "Harris may still be a little suspicious, but he's the only one."

"Well, just be careful, Zeke," said Xad.

Zeke rolled his eyes. "It's fine, Xad."

Meanwhile at Harris's house, his parents wanted to hear all about his visit to Zeke's.

"I hope you were nice to Zeke," said his mom.

"Yeah, no more alien talk," added his dad.

"No, no, we just played some games, that's all," said Harris. *Games from another planet!* he thought. *Even if they were kind of fun . . .*

"Did Zeke's parents tell you anything about Tragas?" asked his dad. "I'm still surprised no one has ever heard of it."

"It's true. They're our new next-door neighbors, but we know so little about them," said his mom.

Harris saw a familiar expression coming across his mom's face. *Uh-oh,* he thought.

"Why don't we invite Zeke and his parents here for dinner?" asked his mom.

"What a great idea!" said his dad.

Harris was shocked. *The aliens . . . here?! Zeke is one thing, but the parents with their odd food and their strange questions? I can't believe Mom is serious!*

"Roxy can come, too," his mom added.

Hmm, Harris thought. *Maybe this isn't a bad thing after all. Maybe seeing Zeke and his parents doing weird stuff at my house, in front of my parents, will be the proof I need to get everyone to realize that Zeke really is an alien.*

"Sounds good, Mom," said Harris.

6 SHOWING OFF

HARRIS WAS LOOKING forward to having Zeke's family over for dinner. This would be his big chance to prove to his parents and Roxy that Zeke was an alien. The dinner was set for the following Saturday.

At school that week, Zeke almost seemed to be showing off.

In gym class, everyone had to climb up a rope. Harris struggled to pull himself even halfway up.

He glanced to his left and saw Zeke scurrying up his rope—with his hands behind his back!

"Wow! That kid sure has strong legs!" said the boy who was climbing the rope to Harris's right. Zeke smiled at Harris on his way down the rope after touching the ceiling.

Is he showing off? Harris wondered. *Could he be getting too confident now that I've been in his house, met his parents, and seen his Tragas technology?*

Later, during arts and crafts, Harris worked on building a birdhouse. He started gluing Popsicle sticks together. As he waited for some of them to dry, he looked over at Zeke and saw that he had already completed a big birdhouse. It had a hole cut in the front, a perch, and a completed roof. Harris had barely begun, and Zeke was already finished.

How did he do that so quickly? Harris wondered.

The next day, Harris was sitting in math class.

"Okay, class, here's your brain-buster problem for the day," said Ms. Milton, their teacher.

She proceeded to write a long list of four-digit numbers on the board. Then she wrote a five-digit number right below it.

"I'd like you to add this list of numbers together, then divide the result by the number on the bottom," said Ms. Milton.

Zeke's hand shot into the air.

"Yes, Zeke. Do you have a question?" asked Ms. Milton.

"No, Ms. Milton. I have the answer," Zeke said.

His fellow students giggled. Zeke looked around, puzzled. Then he told Ms. Milton the answer.

"Why . . . that's correct, Zeke," she said. "Very good! You certainly have a flair for math."

Should I be surprised that an alien's brain works faster than a human's? Harris thought. *I can't wait for Saturday night. Then everyone will finally know.*

THE VERY SPECIAL VISITORS

7

SATURDAY FINALLY CAME.
Harris was excited, but nervous. His parents would finally see for themselves how strange Zeke's family was.

He spent most of the day helping his parents clean the house and set up for dinner.

Roxy came over early to help.

"Now remember, Harris, you need to be on your best behavior," said his mom. "We want Zeke's family to feel welcome in the neighborhood."

"Nothing to worry about, Mom," said Harris, smiling.

Just then, a whistling sound came from outside their front door.

"What in the world is that?" asked Mr. Walker.

Harris remembered Zeke's first day at school. Zeke had whistled outside the classroom door instead of knocking.

"That's Zeke and his parents," Harris explained. "That's how people knock in Tragas!"

Harris opened the door.

"Come in," he said to the three of them as he suspiciously eyed the food they were carrying.

Harris introduced everyone.

"Zeke, these are my parents," Harris said.

"Welcome," said Harris's mom, extending her hand. "Rita and Felix Walker. Nice to meet you."

Zeke's father stared at Mrs. Walker's outstretched hand. "I am Xad, and this is my wife, Quar," he said.

Xad extended his elbow toward Mrs. Walker.

"Um, Dad? People here don't touch elbows as a greeting," Zeke explained. "They shake hands."

"Oh, I'm sorry," said Xad, reaching out and grasping Mrs. Walker's hand firmly before shaking it.

"I kind of like the elbow thing," said Mr. Walker. He extended his elbow and touched Quar's elbow. They both smiled.

"Why don't we have some appetizers in the living room?" said Mr. Walker.

The whole group settled into the living room.

Harris's dad picked up a cracker and placed a slice of cheese on it.

"Cheese and cracker?" he offered Quar.

She took the appetizer and stared at it. When she saw Mr. Walker take a bite, she did the same.

"It tastes kind of sweet and crunchy," said Quar. "I like it. Oh, we brought a delicacy from Tragas to share with you. These are called kreslars."

Xad took the lid off of a platter, revealing what looked like glowing purple slugs.

"Are they raw?" Harris asked, a little grossed out by the slugs' slimy appearance.

"They are, but they don't have to be," replied Xad. "Try one, Harris."

Harris picked up a slug and noticed that steam was now coming off of it. It was warm to the touch.

How did they do that? he wondered. *How did they make it hot?*

"Interesting; they taste kind of like warm fruit," said Mr. Walker.

After trying one, Roxy smiled and looked at Harris. "Not bad, right?"

A buzzer rang in the kitchen, and Harris quickly put his slug back.

"Okay, everybody," Mrs. Walker announced. "Dinner is ready!"

8 DINNER WITH ALIENS!

THE DINNER GUESTS SAT down around the dining room table. Roxy and Harris carried steaming platters of food from the kitchen.

Zeke got up to help.

As Harris put down a platter of fish, he saw Zeke returning from the kitchen. Zeke balanced two bowls, three plates, and a pitcher of water on his arms, shoulders, and head—all quite easily. Harris's parents clapped.

"That's pretty impressive!" said Mr. Walker. Harris put his face in his hands.

"Zeke told us you move around a lot. You must have lived in some interesting places for your work," said Mrs. Walker.

"Oh, yes," said Quar. "In Plaxima, the weather was so severe that we had to walk backward so the wind didn't blow us over. In Jerstik, people could eat their clothing."

"And in Nanstu, the language was so complicated, just saying hello took five minutes," added Xad.

"I've never heard of any of these places," said Mrs. Walker.

"They are pretty far away, and very small," Zeke said quickly, shooting his parents an annoyed look. After all the warnings they gave him about keeping the truth hidden, here *they* were telling strange stories.

As he listened, Harris grew more convinced than ever that Zeke and his parents were aliens. He also noticed that platter after platter of food somehow appeared in front of Zeke and his parents. But he never saw anyone touch or pass anything to anyone else.

I could have sworn those potatoes were in front of Roxy a second ago, and now they're in front of Zeke!

Harris also saw that neither Zeke nor his parents used their utensils. He watched as the food subtly floated up from their plates to their mouths when no one else was looking.

Why doesn't anyone else see this? Harris wondered in frustration.

"What's that?" Roxy asked, pointing to a bottle of orange-and-green liquid that Zeke's parents brought.

"It is Saurlic, a popular beverage in Tragas," explained Xad. "Try some."

Roxy poured herself a glass and took a sip.

"Mmm . . . tastes like a cross between lemonade and orange juice," she said. "I like it." Roxy quickly drank down the whole glass.

Harris looked away for a second to see what Zeke was up to. Zeke was only looking back at him, smiling. When he turned back to Roxy, her empty glass was full again!

How did that happen? he thought. *The bottle is all the way across the room. There is no way anyone could have brought it over, refilled Roxy's glass, then put it back in just a few seconds!*

When dinner ended, Mrs. Walker stood up.

"Let's move to the den for dessert and coffee," she suggested.

9 GROUNDED!

AS HIS PARENTS PREPARED dessert and Harris was walking toward the den, he spotted Zeke's parents in the front hallway. They were both leaning into the coat closet.

"Are you looking for something?" Harris asked.

Quar and Xad turned around quickly. The both looked embarrassed. In reality, they were researching the clothes in the closet. But they couldn't say that to Harris.

Zeke walked in and spoke up. "My parents left the dessert they brought in the closet," he said.

"That's right," said Quar. She reached back into the closet and pulled out a white cake with colorful frosting in a pattern of square shapes.

"Uh, great," said Harris. "You can just bring that into the den."

But Harris was suspicious. *This sounds fishy to me,* he thought. *They never even wore coats and had no reason to go into that closet! Why would they have put a cake in there?*

Harris joined the others in the den. He picked up a knife to cut a piece of the cake and noticed that the squares in the frosting had changed into a series of wavy lines.

Harris looked around. Everyone was chatting, sipping coffee, and happily eating dessert. Zeke and his parents were even using utensils now. It would have seemed perfectly normal if not for everything else Harris had already seen.

*Why does no one but me ever seem
to notice all the strange stuff that
happens around Zeke and his family?* he
wondered. *The appetizer that suddenly
cooked itself, the refilling glass, the
food appearing magically in front of
Zeke, Quar, and Xad, the changing cake
frosting, not to mention everything that
happened at Zeke's house and also at
school. It's all too much. And yet nobody
sees it but me!*

"Well, we would like to thank you for a lovely evening," Quar said when everyone had finished dessert. "But we should be getting home."

Quar, Xad, and Zeke all stood up.

This is it! Harris thought. *My best chance to prove that Zeke's an alien is about to end. I can't take it anymore. I have to convince them. They have to have noticed something. It's now or never!*

Harris stood up.

"That's it! The game is over, Zeke," he announced. "I know that you and your parents are aliens!"

Everyone looked horrified. Roxy looked at Harris and shook her head. Harris's parents jumped up from their seats. "Harris!!!" his mom said.

But Harris continued.

"With all the strange stuff that happened tonight—the floating trays of food, the refilling glass, the steaming appetizer, the—"

Harris's mother cut him off.

"THAT'S ENOUGH!" she shouted.

"Harris. You are grounded. Go to your room right now!"

"But—"

"Now!" his dad said. Defeated, Harris skulked upstairs.

He had his one shot and he blew it. He lingered at the top of the stairs and overhead the rest of the conversation.

"I don't know how to apologize for my son's behavior," said Mr. Walker.

"Don't worry," said Quar. "Our customs in Tragas are very different from yours. Misunderstandings like this happen all the time."

"Well, that's still no excuse for Harris's rudeness," said Mrs. Walker. Then Zeke, Quar, and Xad left the house and headed home.

"Harris just hasn't been his old self since Zeke showed up at school," Roxy said. "I'm worried about him."

"Well, he's lucky to have a friend like you," said Mrs. Walker.

When the cleanup was finished, Roxy went home. This disastrous dinner finally came to an end for all of them.

ZEKE WAS VERY UPSET.

"I can't believe Harris did that!" he said when he and his parents got home. "I knew he had his suspicions, but I never thought he would just blurt it out like that! I shouldn't have pushed him. . . ."

"Don't worry, Zeke," said Quar. "Most humans only believe these things up to a point."

"And even those closest to Harris think he's wrong," added Xad. "Forget about it. It'll go away. Anyway, this was very productive. I think our next research topic might be on strange human foods!"

But Zeke couldn't just let it go.

Harris is my friend, he thought. *And now he's in trouble, just because he was able to figure out the truth. I really like Harris. He and Roxy were the first kids to be really nice to me at school. Even if he was only nice to me to prove that I'm an alien, we have fun together, right? I feel terrible about this. And now Harris is grounded for who knows how long? But he wasn't wrong! He doesn't deserve to be in trouble.*

And I'm going to do something about it!

Harris remained grounded for the time being. He went to school each day, but then he had to come right home. He couldn't see his friends. He wasn't even allowed to talk to Roxy on the phone. And he was worried about what she must have thought of him after what happened.

A few days later at the dinner table, Harris said to his parents, "I apologize for being rude to our guests on Saturday."

"And are you ready to admit that what you said is nonsense?" asked his mother.

Harris stayed silent.

"Well then, it's back to your room as soon as you're finished with dinner," said his father.

The next day after school, Harris was stuck in his room as usual. He was bored. He had nothing to do except think about Zeke. Even his favorite comic books were taken away by his parents.

He rolled over on his bed and glanced out the window. There was Zeke floating in midair, two stories up!

Harris leapt from his bed and rubbed his eyes. When he opened them, Zeke was gone. He rushed to his window and looked outside, but there was nothing there.

"What the . . . ?"

Harris turned around and jumped up in surprise. Zeke was standing behind him, right there in Harris's room.

"How did you get in here?" Harris asked. "Is this even real? Am I dreaming? Have I lost my mind?"

"No, Harris," said Zeke. "You are awake . . . and sane. Well, as far as I know," Zeke said with a smile. "And you're correct."

"Correct?" asked Harris.

"My family and I really are aliens from the *planet* Tragas," Zeke admitted. "You are my friend, and I couldn't let you be grounded anymore for figuring out the truth."

Harris gasped and said, "I *knew* it!"

"My parents and I do move from place to place," Zeke explained. "But it is from planet to planet. I'm always the new kid. And I'm always 'different.' But you wanted to be my friend anyway."

"I don't know what to say," said Harris. "I'm glad you trust me. And am also glad I'm not crazy!"

"And now I must ask you to help me keep my secret," said Zeke. "Most people on Earth wouldn't be as welcoming as you."

"I will," Harris promised. "As long as you promise you're not one of those evil aliens I always see in the movies."

Zeke laughed and said, "Most of the time. I promise."

Zeke levitated into the air and floated out the window.

Harris raced downstairs.

"Mom! Dad!" he called out. "I have something to tell you."

His parents met him at the bottom of the stairs.

"I want to apologize," he said.

"I admit that I have an overactive imagination. I let it get the better of me. Of course Zeke and his parents aren't aliens. That was dumb. You'll never hear me mention it again."

"Well, I'm very glad to hear you say that, Harris," said his dad. "I think you can officially consider yourself un-grounded now."

His mom nodded in agreement. "As long as you go upstairs and call Zeke and his parents to apologize to them. And after that, call Roxy. You owe her an apology, too."

"I'll do it right now," said Harris.

He bounded up the stairs, excited by this new chance to help his new friend Zeke *keep* his secret rather than trying to expose it.

I was right! My next-door neighbor is actually an alien! He looked out his window where Zeke had been floating just a few minutes before and thought, *How cool is that?!*

THE ALIEN NEXT DOOR

ALIEN SCOUT

BY A. I. NEWTON   ILLUSTRATED BY ANJAN SARKAR

3

TABLE OF CONTENTS

1 A FRIEND'S SECRET

HARRIS WALKER AND HIS FRIEND ZEKE were sprawled out on the floor of Harris's bedroom, reading comic books. Harris loved showing off his collection.

"Now this one is called *Invaders From Beyond*," Harris said. "It's about these aliens from another dimension who can travel through time and shoot power beams from their eyes that can blow up entire mountains."

Zeke looked at his friend and laughed.

"You don't really believe all this stuff is true, do you?" he asked.

Harris laughed, too.

"Well, *you* can do some pretty amazing things, can't you?" he asked.

A lot had changed in the friendship between the two next-door neighbors since Zeke finally admitted the truth to Harris—Zeke was an alien from the planet Tragas!

"Yeah, but not *that* amazing," said Zeke. "Traveling through time and blowing up mountains is a bit beyond my skills."

"Okay, so what *can* you actually do?" Harris asked. "I mean, I know you can float, you can project what you see in your head onto screens, and you can heat stuff up with your hands."

"Let's see," Zeke said. "I can also move objects with my mind."

The next page in the comic book page turned over all by itself, revealing a picture of an alien lifting an entire building with one hand.

"Well, I definitely can't do *that*!"
Zeke said.

Both boys laughed.

The next morning, Harris sat on the school bus next to Zeke.

"I just found out that I'm going on a camping weekend with the Beaver Scouts," Harris said excitedly.

"Beaver Scouts?" Zeke asked.

"They run this camp, and every October, boys can go there for a long weekend," Harris explained.

"I've heard people talk about it for years. In fact, my dad went when he was a kid. And this year *I* finally get to go! We'll get to do all kinds of cool stuff—go canoeing, pitching a tent, and even telling scary stories at night!"

"And these things are fun?" Zeke asked.

Before Harris could answer, his best friend Roxy joined them on the bus.

"Well, you look pretty happy," she said to Harris.

"He is going to something called . . . Beaver Scout Camp," Zeke explained, still not quite sure what it was all about.

"So your parents finally think you're old enough to go? " asked Roxy. "Congratulations! I know how much you've looked forward to this. Is Zeke going, too?"

"No," replied Harris. *Actually, I don't think I know anyone who's going*, he thought to himself.

When the bus arrived at school, Harris pulled Zeke aside after they got off.

"Why don't you see if you can come with me to the camp?" he blurted out.

Even though he was excited, Harris was a little nervous about going off to camp and not knowing anyone else who'd be there.

"It'll be really fun, I promise, and a great way to learn about Earth kids!" said Harris.

"I guess it might be. . . ." said Zeke.
"I'll talk it over with my parents."

CAMPER ZEKE

THAT EVENING, ZEKE TOLD his parents about Beaver Scout Camp.

"Floating on the water? Sleeping in the outdoors? Scaring people with words? Why are these things fun?" asked his mom, Quar.

"I'm not really sure," Zeke admitted. "But Harris seems very excited about going. And he asked me to come along with him."

Zeke's dad, Xad, was happy that Zeke was fitting in here on Earth.

Each time he and Quar moved to a new planet, Zeke found it difficult to start over at a new school and make new friends.

"This could be a good thing, Zeke," Xad said. "You will learn more about how Earth kids behave. And it will really help our research!"

"I am a little concerned," said Quar. "Ever since you met him, Harris has been trying to prove that you are an alien. I'm afraid that spending so much time together might make it harder for you to keep our secret."

Zeke had decided not to tell his parents that Harris now knew the truth about Zeke being an alien. Zeke decided to trust him.

"I am not worried about that, Quar," Zeke said. "Harris apologized, and I think everyone was able to convince him that we aren't aliens."

"Okay, I guess it will be okay then," said Quar. "But be careful."

"I'm not sure I will have a good time doing all these strange Earth things," Zeke said. "But I do like the idea of spending time with Harris. Okay then, I'll go."

Zeke called Harris with the news.

"That's fantastic!" Harris cried. "We are going to have the best time ever!"

Well, I sure hope so, thought Zeke.

OFF TO CAMP

ON A CRISP OCTOBER MORNING, Zeke and his parents gathered with Harris and his parents in the driveway next to the Walkers' house. Roxy was also there to see them off.

"I believe that Zeke has all the necessary supplies," said Quar. "He has his emergency transmitter."

"It's called a cell phone," Zeke explained.

"And his nutrition-infusion packets," Quar continued.

"They're called energy bars," Zeke said.

"Oh, don't worry," said Harris's dad. "There's always plenty of food for the campers. When I went as a kid, we had a cookout every night!"

"I think it's so cool that you two are going together," said Roxy.

"Thanks, Roxy," said Zeke. "I wish you could come, too."

"Oh, don't worry about me," Roxy said. "I'm going to see a soccer game this weekend with my cousin Rebecca. You two just have a great time!"

"We will try," said Zeke.

"Well, don't make it sound like work," Harris said. "It's going to be fun!"

"Time to go," said Harris's mom. "We don't want to be late for the bus."

Zeke lifted a white, egg-shaped container from off his front lawn and placed it in the back of the car.

"What that?" Roxy asked.

"It's my travel pod," Zeke explained. "It holds my belongings."

"Oh, you mean your suitcase," said Harris.

Zeke, Harris, and Harris's parents climbed into the car and drove away.

"Bye!" yelled Roxy.

Zeke's parents waved. Harris thought they looked a little worried.

"Okay, let's make sure you have everything, Harris," said his mom. "Eight pairs of socks, right?"

"Yes, Mom."

"Five bathing suits, right?"

"Mom, we—"

"Three bottles each of sunscreen and bug spray, right?"

"Mom, we went over this four times in the house!" Harris said.

"I know, honey, but this is your first time away from home alone," said Mom.

"He'll be fine," said Harris's dad. "I remember all the wacky stuff I did when I was a camper. We had contests to see who could get their marshmallow the blackest and still be able to eat it. We stayed up all night on the trip playing games. Oh, and we climbed the tallest tree in the county. Wait until you get a load of this tree!"

A short while later, the car pulled into a parking lot. Kids streamed from their parents' cars and climbed on board the bus that would bring the campers to Beaver Scouts camp.

"Have a great time, Harris!" said his mom, hugging him. "You too, Zeke."

The boys grabbed their gear from the car and headed for the bus.

"I'm really glad you're coming with me, Zeke," Harris said, as the two boys stepped onto the bus.

4 ALL ABOARD

THE BUS WAS FILLED with a large group of laughing, screaming kids. Harris could feel the excitement.

For Zeke, the noisy bus reminded him of the sad feeling he had when he stepped onto the school bus just a few weeks earlier as the new kid at Jefferson Elementary School.

But the feeling passed. This time, he had a friend at his side.

As the bus pulled out of the parking lot, Patrick, the head counselor, stood up and got everyone's attention to be quiet.

"Welcome, Beaver Scouts!" he said with a big smile. "You are in for a great weekend! We'll be playing games and sports, going on an overnight camping trip in the woods, all kinds of totally cool stuff. Just sit back and relax, and we'll be there in a few hours."

Zeke looked out the window and watched the scenery change from large, family houses and shopping malls to scattered trees and farm fields. Soon, mountains came into view.

BANG!

A loud boom sounded and jolted the bus. It pulled over to the side of the road, then rumbled to a stop.

The driver and Patrick ran outside
to investigate. A few seconds later,
Patrick stuck his head back in as the
driver grabbed a toolbox.

"Sit tight, everybody," he said. "We
have a flat tire. I'll check it out."

"Oh, great!" moaned one boy. "Stuck
here in the middle of nowhere!"

"What about this air pump?" Patrick asked the driver, pointing at it among the tools.

The driver shook his head.

"It's no good," said the driver. "There's a hole in the tire. I'll have to put on the spare tire, which will take a while. We're going to be late, I'm afraid." The two men got back on the bus to call the camp to let them know.

Zeke quietly got up and slipped out of the bus amid the commotion.

"Hey! Where are you going?" Harris followed, wondering what in the world Zeke was doing.

Outside, Harris watched Zeke kneel beside the flat tire. Zeke looked back toward the sky, and then he cupped his hands around the hole. Suddenly, they started to glow bright red.

"What are you doing?!" Harris whispered to Zeke, looking around, worried that someone might catch Zeke using his powers.

"I'm redirecting energy from the Earth's sun through my hands to heat the rubber enough so it'll melt and seal the hole in the tire," Zeke explained as casually as if he were telling Harris what he had brought for lunch.

A moment later, the bus driver stepped outside.

"What's going on out here?" he asked.

Zeke stood up.

"There is no longer a hole in the tire," Zeke explained. "You may now fill it using the air pump."

The driver knelt down and looked at the tire, astonished. Then he looked up at Zeke.

"He studied auto repair at his last school," Harris explained. "He's very talented."

The driver gave Zeke a funny look, then shrugged and pumped the tire full of air.

"You'll have to be careful this weekend around everyone," Harris whispered to Zeke when they got back to their seats. "We need to keep your secret safe!"

Zeke smiled. He was glad he had Harris to help him keep his secret.

5 BEAVER SCOUTS CAMP

THE BUS BOUNCED ALONG
a bumpy country road surrounded
by tall trees.

"Maybe that kid was right," Harris
said to Zeke. "I think we really are in
the middle of nowhere."

Zeke looked puzzled.

"How can anyone be nowhere?" he asked. "We are always, actually somewhere, wherever that may be."

Harris laughed. "That's true, but it's just an expression for a really far-away place."

The bus turned onto an even narrower, bumpier dirt road.

"I take it back," said Harris. "I think *this* is officially the middle of nowhere."

The bus rolled through a large entry gate. Above the gate swung an old wooden sign with the image of a beaver carved into it. The trees opened up into a clearing, and they passed a lake with a waterfall falling into it.

Harris got very excited. "I love being in the woods," he said.

Zeke looked puzzled again. "We have woods on Tragas, but nothing like this," he explained. "The trees are striped, the lakes are yellow, and the waterfalls flow *up*, not down."

The bus rolled to a stop in front of a flagpole in the center of a circle of cabins. Patrick stood up and spoke.

"Okay, listen up. They'll be four scouts to a cabin. Listen for your name and cabin assignment."

Patrick then read the names of all the campers and their cabin numbers.

"Cabin five—Harris, Zeke, Roger, and Paul," Patrick announced.

"That's us," said Harris, grabbing his backpack and heading off the bus.

Harris and Zeke walked into the spare wooden cabin. On either side were a pair of bunk beds. A few seconds later, two more boys came in.

"I'm Roger," said a tall, thin boy with red hair. "And this is my friend, Paul."

Harris recognized Paul as the kid who had complained about being in the middle of nowhere. Paul was short with curly brown hair.

"I'm Harris, and this is my friend, Zeke," said Harris.

Roger and Paul went to one of the bunk beds. Harris and Zeke walked over to the other.

"Would you prefer the top bed or the bottom?" Harris asked Zeke.

Without answering Harris's question, Zeke used his powers to float up into the top bunk.

"I guess that answers my question," Harris said. "I'm actually glad since I'm kind of afraid of heights."

"Whoa, how did you get up there so fast?" Paul asked from across the room. He pointed to Zeke, who sat on the top bunk.

"Zeke's a great climber," Harris said quickly. "You should see how fast he climbs up a rope!" Zeke laughed.

Roger smiled and nodded at Zeke. Paul narrowed his eyes, then went back to unpacking.

This Paul kid could be trouble, Harris thought. *Zeke will have to be extra careful around him.*

A whistle sounded from outside the cabin.

"Everyone to the flagpole!" Patrick shouted.

Camp was about to begin!

6
CANOE ADVENTURE

"OKAY, EVERYONE, LISTEN UP!"
Patrick shouted as the campers gathered around. "In a few minutes, we'll head over to the mess hall for lunch."

"*Mess* hall?" Zeke whispered to Harris. "I've always been told not to make a mess with food."

Harris smiled. "It's just another word for the place where we eat," he explained.

Patrick continued. "After lunch, we'll meet at the river to teach you how to canoe and take a trip down the river. So . . . welcome to Beaver Scouts Camp!"

In the mess hall, Harris and Zeke sat with Roger and Paul.

"So, where are you guys from?" Roger asked.

"We both go to Jefferson Elementary School," Harris said quickly, hoping to avoid any talk about Zeke's true home.

"I'm originally from Tragas," said Zeke.

He really didn't have to say that! Harris thought.

"Tragas?" said Paul. "Where's that? Never even heard of it."

"It's pretty far from here," Zeke replied.

Harris quickly changed the subject. "I really like playing soccer," he said.

"Me too," said Roger. "I love soccer!"

But Paul eyed Zeke suspiciously.

After lunch, the campers all gathered at the river and began their canoe lessons.

Harris and Zeke put on their life vests and climbed into an available canoe. Roger and Paul got into another. They launched their canoes into the river. Harris paddled gently. They moved smoothly through the calm, flowing water.

"Hey!" Paul shouted from the canoe behind Harris and Zeke's. "How can they be that far ahead of us with only one kid paddling?"

Harris turned around and saw Zeke holding his paddle in his lap. But the water on either side of him was churning, pushing the canoe quickly down the river.

"You actually have to put your paddle in the water, Zeke!" Harris whispered. Then he shouted, "Paddle harder, Zeke!"

"Why?" Zeke asked Harris. "We move faster if I use mind projection to push the boat through the water."

"Do I have to remind you that you asked me to help you keep your powers a secret?" Harris asked softly.

Zeke sighed. "You're right," he said. "I will be more careful."

Zeke dipped his paddle into the river and moved it through the water. *Gosh, this is so much harder!* Zeke thought.

Roger and Paul slipped ahead of them.

"Hey, we're leading!" Roger said.

But Paul just glared at Zeke as they passed.

A short while later, the river split into two branches. To the right, it remained calm. But to the left, the water looked choppy and picked up speed very quickly.

"Everyone, steer right!" Patrick shouted.

But as they reached the fork, Roger and Paul had trouble steering their canoe. They were pulled to the left, into the fast, rushing current.

"Help!" Paul cried. "We went the wrong way!"

Roger panicked. He stood up in the canoe to try to get more power from his paddle, but he tumbled overboard into the churning, swirling current!

"Roger!" Paul screamed, looking down into the water.

RESCUE!

HARRIS WAS REALLY WORRIED.
He saw Patrick paddling hard toward
the spot where Roger had fallen in.
Paul managed to grab an overhanging
tree branch and pull his canoe safely
to shore.

Harris felt his own boat suddenly zoom through the water back toward the fork. He turned and saw Zeke sitting quietly with his eyes closed. Their canoe cut through the rushing current like a motorboat.

Zeke is using his powers! Harris thought. *I hope he doesn't get caught, but he may be the only one who can get to Roger in time!*

When they reached the spot where Roger fell in, Zeke dove out of the canoe. He disappeared down into the bubbling water.

Harris paddled as hard as he could, fighting the current, and made it to the shore. He stared into the rushing water.

Come on! Come on! he thought.

Just as Patrick's canoe arrived, Zeke burst through the surface of the water with Roger in his arms. He helped Roger into the canoe, then climbed in after him. He and Patrick paddled hard to the riverbank as Zeke secretly moved their boat along using his powers.

Once they all got to shore, they carried their canoes over to the calm part of the river.

"You're quite a swimmer, Zeke," Patrick said once everyone was safely on shore.

Zeke looked puzzled. "I can't swim," he said, being completely serious.

Wow! Harris thought. *He must have used his floating power to move him through the water. So he wasn't actually swimming!*

Everyone laughed, thinking this was a joke.

"Thanks, Zeke," said Roger once he had caught his breath.

"Yeah, thanks for rescuing my friend," Paul added.

But Harris noticed a suspicious look on Paul's face, even as he was thanking Zeke.

After the canoe trip, the campers gathered for lunch.

"How are you feeling?" Harris asked Roger as they ate.

"Good as new, thanks to Zeke," Roger replied, patting Zeke on the back.

Zeke smiled. He felt like he had just made another human friend.

"Don't forget," Patrick announced as the campers finished lunch, "tomorrow we go on our overnight camp-out!"

8 SETTING UP CAMP

ON THE WAY BACK TO THEIR bunk, Harris explained to Zeke what a campout was.

"Why would we sleep outside when we have a perfectly fine bunk bed in the cabin?" Zeke asked.

"Because it's fun!" Harris replied.
Zeke shrugged. "I guess it's just
one more Earth thing I really don't
understand."

The next morning, the campers gathered at the flagpole. They each had a backpack full of gear.

"Okay, campers. Remember, no cell phones or other devices," Patrick announced. "Leave them in your bunks. We are going into the great outdoors, back to a time before technology. Follow me!"

A line of campers followed Patrick onto a path that led deep into the woods. After hiking for about an hour, they came to a clearing. In the center was a fire pit made of stones.

"Okay, we made it! Wasn't that fun? Now we have to set up your tents in a circle around the fire pit," said Patrick.

Harris and Zeke pulled out their tent, placed it onto the ground, then crawled inside with the tent poles to set it up.

"I think that one goes over there, Zeke," said Harris, shoving a pole into the center of the tent.

Zeke stuck one end of a tent pole into the ground, then shoved the other end into a small pocket in the canvas flaps. But the pole popped out and poked Harris right in the butt.

Then the whole tent collapsed on top of them.

Both boys cracked up.

"Even though I've never done this before, I don't think we're doing it right," said Zeke.

Harris stuck his head out to see how the other campers were doing. Some were almost finished. Others, including Roger and Paul, were also struggling.

"You know, Zeke, no one is watching us," Harris said. "They're all busy trying to set up their own tents. So, um . . ."

Harris didn't have to finish his sentence. Zeke smiled and closed his eyes. He spread his hands wide apart, and the tent poles lifted into place perfectly. Then the canvas drifted down onto the poles until the tent was fully built and ready to use.

"You know, normally I would tell you to be more careful with your powers, but this was so much less annoying than building the thing piece by piece," Harris said. "I just hope no one noticed."

The boys crawled out from their tent to see Roger and Paul still struggling with theirs.

"Hey, how did you put that tent up so fast?" asked Paul, as a tent flap dropped down and covered his face.

"Camping is one of my favorite activities back in Tragas," Zeke said quickly. "I think it's so much fun to sleep outdoors 'in the middle of nowhere.'"

Harris turned away, afraid that if he looked Zeke in the eyes, he would crack up laughing.

When the sun went down, Patrick lit a roaring campfire. All the campers gathered around the blaze. They stuck hot dogs on sticks and roasted them over the fire.

After dinner, Patrick asked, "Who wants a marshmallow?" as he opened a huge bag.

Harris took a marshmallow, slid it onto a stick, and held it over the fire.

Zeke took a marshmallow from the bag. As he went to put it into his mouth, Harris noticed that the marshmallow was fully toasted.

"But you didn't even hold it over the fire first," Harris said, looking around to see if anyone else had also seen this.

"Why bother?" Zeke asked. "If the point is to heat the marshmallow, I can do that with my hands."

"But that takes all the fun out of it," Harris insisted.

"Fun like sleeping outdoors?" Zeke asked.

Harris laughed. *They just must have a different definition of fun on Tragas!* he thought.

The full moon rose above the blazing campfire.

"Kind of spooky out here, right? It feels like a perfect night for scary stories!" said Patrick.

"I've got a scary one," said Paul. Then he stood up and began.

9 SCARY TALES

BY THE FLICKERING GLOW of the campfire, Paul told the story of a brother and sister who were dared to go into an old, run-down shack in the woods near their town.

Kids in the nearby town thought it was haunted. Their parents told them that this wasn't true and that no one had lived there for decades, but the shack always seemed to have had a small, flickering light glowing inside of it. Whenever the kids walked by it, they always tried to get one another to knock on the door.

One night, the brother and sister finally took the dare. Deep in the dark, creepy woods, they found the vine-covered shack and knocked on the creaky door.

"It's open," said a raspy voice from inside.

The two kids looked at each other in shock, gulped, then opened the door and stepped into the shack. They pushed past cobwebs and sidestepped scurrying rats.

At the far end of the room in the dark sat a woman. Suddenly, she lit a candle, and in the light, they could see her warty, wrinkled skin. Her wispy white hair circled her head like smoke, and she smiled at them, revealing yellow, rotten teeth.

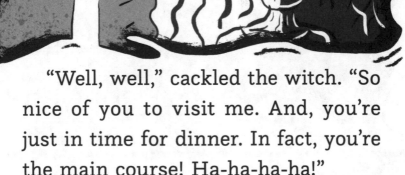

"Well, well," cackled the witch. "So nice of you to visit me. And, you're just in time for dinner. In fact, you're the main course! Ha-ha-ha-ha!"

The kids screamed and dashed from the house. As they ran through the woods, they could still hear the witch's hideous laughter.

They finally arrived at home, and burst through the front door.

"Mom! Dad! We're home!" they shouted, but then they stopped in their tracks.

There, standing in the hallway, was the witch!

"So, you've decided to have dinner at home," the witch said. "Excellent. In fact, I just finished eating my appetizers, though you know them as Mom and Dad!"

The door closed behind them, and they were never heard from again.

Paul finished and sat down. A few kids squirmed, and others laughed.

"I have a scary story, too," Zeke announced.

Harris was surprised, and a little worried.

Zeke stood up and launched into the story of the Kraka Beast of Tragas, a monster that eats trees and destroys buildings. Zeke told a tale of the destruction of an entire city by the beast.

"That's not as scary as my story," said Paul.

"Maybe, but mine is true!" said Zeke. Everyone laughed.

"So is mine!" said Paul jokingly.

"Forget it," whispered Harris. "*I* believe you."

The fire died down.

"Time to hit the hay," announced Paul. "Everyone go back to their tents."

Why would I want to hit hay? thought Zeke as they returned to their tents.

The next morning, the campers got up with the sunrise. They packed up their tents and started the hike back to the cabins. Along the way, Paul, Roger, Harris, and Zeke came to a stop at a very tall tree.

Paul pointed up at the tree. "You're supposed to be a good climber, right, Zeke?" he asked. "I bet I can climb that tree higher and faster than you or anybody else here."

"Not me," said Roger. "My mom's calling soon, so I have to get back to the cabin. See you guys back there." Roger continued along the trail. Harris looked up at the tree. *This must be the tree that Dad climbed when he was a camper,* he thought. *Only Dad isn't afraid of heights!*

10 THE CLIMB

ZEKE AND PAUL STARTED CLIMBING.
They both moved quickly up the tree.

This would be so much easier if I could just use my powers, Zeke thought.

Harris really wanted to climb the tree, but he just couldn't seem to make himself walk over to it and begin.

Zeke glanced down and saw that Harris was still standing on the ground. He looked up at Paul, who was reaching for a branch high above him.

Zeke climbed back down.

"Let's climb together, okay?" Zeke asked.

Harris took a deep breath and stepped onto the lowest branch.

"Just go slowly, Harris," Zeke said. "I won't let anything happen to you."

Harris nodded and slowly made his way up the tree. He had only gotten a little way up when he heard Paul's voice from above.

"I beat both of you! Look at me!" Paul shouted from the highest branch. "I'm king of the tree!"

Paul raised his arms to the sky in victory, but somehow lost his balance and fell. He plunged toward the ground below.

"Aaahhh!" he cried.

Harris looked up helplessly and winced. There was nothing he could do to help.

Zeke closed his eyes and focused on Paul. He had to use his powers, but he couldn't be too obvious about it.

Zeke slowed Paul down a bit until he was just two feet from the ground, then he let Paul hit the ground at normal speed.

Climbing down quickly, Zeke and Harris rushed to Paul's side and helped him to his feet.

"Are you all right?" asked Harris.

"Yeah," said Paul, dazed. "It was weird. As I was falling, I felt like something was holding me, even slowing me down. I'm not sure exactly what happened. It's kind of a blur."

Then he paused, and looked right at Zeke. "Hey, um . . thanks," he said quietly.

"You're welcome," Zeke replied, flashing a sly smile. "But I'm not sure what you're thanking me for."

The following morning, the campers all boarded the bus for home.

"So what did you think of camp?" Harris asked Zeke during their ride.

"Interesting," Zeke said. "I still can't say that I understand humans that well, but I did actually have a good time with you."

When the bus arrived, Harris's parents were waiting for them, along with Roxy.

"How was it?" Roxy asked on the car ride home.

Zeke and Harris took turns telling stories about their adventures.

"Well, we're just glad that Harris got to go with a friend," said his mom.

"So," Roxy said, smiling. "See any aliens at camp?"

"Only this guy," Harris said, pointing at Zeke. Everyone laughed, believing that Harris was just kidding, making fun of himself for the way he used to think that Harris was an alien.

"Well," Zeke spoke up, "there *were* a couple of kids there that I wasn't too sure about!"

Harris smiled, happy that, at least for the moment, Zeke's secret was still safe.

THE ALIEN NEXT DOOR

TRICK OR CHEAT?

BY A. I. NEWTON   ILLUSTRATED BY ANJAN SARKAR   4

TABLE OF CONTENTS

HALLOWEEN'S COMING

HARRIS WALKER RUSHED NEXT
door to his friend Zeke's house on
Sunday. Harris and Zeke had only
been home for a week following their
adventure at Beaver Scouts camp, but
already it felt like a million years ago.
Halloween was coming this week, and
that was all Harris could think about.

"Guess what?" Harris asked excitedly when he joined Zeke in his room. "It's almost Halloween!"

"Hall-o-what?" Zeke asked, repeating the unfamiliar word.

Harris smiled. He had become such good friends with Zeke that sometimes he forgot that his next door neighbor was not from Earth.

"They don't have Halloween on Tragas?!" Harris asked.

"Correct," said Zeke. "What is it?"

"Everyone dresses up in costumes," Harris explained. "For that one day, you can be whatever you want to be—a ghost, a monster, an animal, an object. Anything you can imagine! Then we all go trick-or-treating."

"What does that mean?" Zeke asked.

"We go from house to house and get candy," Harris said. "And the whole neighborhood is decorated with ghosts and cobwebs and other spooky stuff. Then we come home, watch scary movies, and eat our candy. It's the *best* holiday!"

Zeke looked puzzled. "So, once again, like when we were telling scary stories around the campfire on our scouting trip, we *want* to get scared because it's . . . fun?"

"Exactly!" Harris said. "Now you get it."

"I'm still not sure I do," Zeke said. "But I want to learn all I can about Earth culture. And I do appreciate you helping me make my way through your strange customs."

"Oh, and I almost forgot the best part," Harris continued. "Every year at school, we have a costume contest! All the kids and teachers dress up in Halloween costumes, and then the kids compete to see who has best costume."

"I'm not sure why people would want to dress up in costumes," Zeke said. "But I do like competitions. Back on Tragas, we had contests to see who could levitate the heaviest load, or who could navigate a pebble through a bunch of moving rings."

"That sounds really cool! Do you know what you want your costume to be?" Harris asked.

Zeke smiled. "Well, If I understand you correctly about this costume contest, I don't think I need a costume at all," he said.

Harris was confused. "What do you mean?" he asked.

"I'll just go as myself!" Zeke announced.

HARRIS WAS VERY CONFUSED.

How can Zeke go as himself for Halloween? He may be an alien, but he just looks like a normal kid.

Zeke smiled. "I do indeed understand. There's something I haven't told you about myself yet," he said.

I know that he's an alien. I know he comes from the planet Tragas and that he has some pretty cool powers. But what hasn't he told me? Harris wondered.

"The way I look," Zeke began. "I mean the way I look now, like a human, that's not the way I really look."

"I'm not sure you understood what I said about dressing up for Halloween," he said. "The whole point is to *not* look like yourself, to dress up as something different, or something funny, or scary."

"What do you mean?" Harris asked, more confused than ever.

"My human appearance is only a disguise," Zeke explained. "People from Tragas have the ability to change our appearance. We can make ourselves look like the inhabitants of whatever planet we're currently on. This is very useful when my parents and I move from planet to planet for their research. It allows us to blend in."

Harris had to sit down. Somehow, this was even more shocking to him than learning that his new friend really was an alien.

"So, if this is not what you really look like," he asked, "what *do* you really look like?"

"I'll show you," said Zeke.

Zeke took a deep breath and raised his arms above his head. His body started to vibrate, then glow with a faintly yellow gleam. His skin and features softened into wavy lines, and then he began to grow taller and taller.

Harris looked up in amazement as Zeke completely changed shape.

The yellow glow faded, revealing Zeke's purple skin. His human arms disappeared, replaced by six tentacles extending out from his shoulders. His human facial features completely vanished. His ears were two antennae pointing up from the sides of his face. His hair disappeared, revealing a bald green head.

He had no legs, and was floating above the ground. His five eyes all were looking at Harris.

Harris was stunned. He couldn't believe that this was what his friend really looked like!

"It's still me, Harris," Zeke said. His voice was unchanged. "I'm still the same Zeke."

"Um, not exactly," Harris said. Then both boys cracked up laughing.

"You know what I mean," said Zeke.

Harris smiled in wonder. "Hot dog!" he suddenly exclaimed.

Zeke looked confused. "What does any of this have to do with the beef shaped like a log that we cooked up at the campfire at scout camp?" he asked.

"Hah, it's just an Earth expression," Harris explained.

Zeke nodded, then quickly transformed back into his human form.

"Well, *you* obviously don't need to make a costume," said Harris. "Just go as your true self, and you'll win easily! I've never come close to winning!"

"What was your costume last year?" Zeke asked.

"I was a superhero, but this year, I want to be a robot," Harris said.

Zeke thought for a moment, then smiled.

"I have an idea," he said. "And if it works, you'll have the best costume!"

THE BEST ROBOT EVER

THE TWO FRIENDS HEADED downstairs to the workshop in the basement of Zeke's house. Large metal tubes, electric wires, and weird-looking circuits were spread all over the floor and workbench.

319

"What's all this?" Harris asked.

"My dad and I like to tinker with some of the Tragas technology we brought from home," Zeke explained. "I'm pretty good at building stuff."

Zeke levitated some long metal tubes, some flashing bulbs, and a whole bunch of wires above their heads. Harris watched in amazement, and his friend got to work assembling them in the air.

As he finished each section, Zeke lowered the completed metal pieces onto Harris. More and more, Harris began to look like a robot.

The robot's body was a square box cut to fit tightly against Harris's own body, complete with blinking dials and knobs. The arms and legs were metal stovepipes attached to his body. For the head, Zeke used what looked like an old TV. He attached a small metal rod to look like a bright antenna.

"Pretty good," said Zeke, stepping back and looking at his creation.

"I want to see!" Harris rushed back up to Zeke's room and looked into a mirror.

"Wow!" he said. "This is amazing. I really look like a robot!"

When Harris turned around, he saw that Zeke had again transformed into his true alien body.

"But I still think you're going to win the contest, Zeke," he said.

Downstairs, the front doorbell rang. Zeke's mother called up to them: "Zeke, Harris, your friend Roxy is here!" she shouted.

Harris froze. "Oh, no!" Harris said. "This is bad, this is really, really bad!"

"I don't understand," Zeke said. "Usually you are happy to see Roxy."

Harris heard footsteps bounding up the stairs.

"There's no time to explain, but Roxy is going to be so mad," Harris said.

A few seconds later, the door swung open. Roxy started talking before she was even in the room.

"Harris, I called your house and your mother said you were at Zeke's, so I rushed right over. I have such a cool idea for our Halloween costumes this year," she said, stepping into the room. "Wait 'til you hear this. I—"

Roxy stopped short at the sight of Harris in his robot costume and Zeke in his alien "costume."

"I can't believe you made your costumes *without me*!" she cried.

4 ROXY'S REACTION

ROXY GLARED AT HARRIS, shaking her head. "Harris! We *always* do our costumes together!"

"I'm really sorry, Roxy," Harris said. He removed his robot head. "I was just teaching Zeke about Halloween, since they don't have it on Tragas. Then I told him about the costume contest, and he helped me with my costume, so I—uh—helped him with his, and this just kind of happened."

I wish I could tell her about Zeke, but I can't. I promised.

"You know, it's not very nice of you to leave me out," Roxy continued. "I'm happy that you and Zeke have become friends."

"Me too," said Zeke, turning two of his five eyeballs toward Roxy.

"But where does that leave *me*?" she asked.

"What do you mean?" Harris asked, starting to feel a bit ridiculous having a serious conversation while still in his robot costume. "We're still friends, Roxy. Just because I'm friends with Zeke doesn't mean we're not still friends."

"You two go to camp together, you make your costumes together, when you know we always do that together."

"Yeah, but—"

But Roxy wasn't finished.

"And don't forget, Harris," she continued, "that *I* was the one who was friendly to Zeke first. *I* had to convince you to be friends with him. You were too busy trying to prove that he was an alien."

Harris and Zeke remained silent.

She's not really wrong about any of this, Harris thought. *Even if I was right about Zeke!*

"I'm sorry, Roxy," Harris said. "I really am. I didn't think."

Roxy walked toward the door. She stopped, turned back, and looked at Zeke.

"Nice alien costume, Zeke," she said. "You better watch out or Harris might turn you in for being a real alien."

Then she turned and left.

Once Roxy had gone, Zeke changed back into his human form.

"Did I do something wrong?" he asked Harris.

"I don't think so," Harris replied. "Every year since we were little, Roxy and I have made our costumes together. I guess I was so stunned by seeing what you really look like and excited about how you could make  my costume, Roxy never crossed my mind. I never meant to leave her out. I just lost track of everything."

"Maybe Roxy can dress up in a costume that goes with ours," Zeke suggested. "Then we can all go treat-tricking together."

"It's trick-or-treating, but yes, I think that's a good idea."

Harris felt better, but he worried that Roxy might not want to go trick-or-treating with him. And he was sad that for the first time since before he could remember, he and Roxy didn't work on their costumes together.

5 COSTUME DAY

ON WEDNESDAY, THE HALLOWEEN
costume contest finally arrived. All
the kids excitedly streamed into
school in their costumes. The halls
and classrooms were filled with
witches, goblins, vampires, zombies,
werewolves, mummies, cowboys,
pirates, princesses, ghosts, ninjas, and
animals of all types.

Harris clanked his way into school wearing his robot costume. Zeke came in behind him, displaying his true alien form in public for the first time since he arrived on Earth.

As soon as Zeke entered the school, he could see kids pointing at him.

"It's a little scary but actually kind of fun to be out in public in my true form," Zeke whispered to Harris.

"Don't worry," Harris said. "Just keep pretending that it's a costume. Nobody will suspect it's real."

"Wow! That's the best alien costume I've ever seen," said a girl dressed like a zombie. "How are you floating like that?"

"Uh, there's hover technology built into the bottom of the costume, obviously!" said Harris.

"You are *so* going to win the contest," said a boy dressed like lion.

"Thank you. I think Harris has a cool costume, too," Zeke said, pointing two of his tentacles at Harris.

"Whoa, nice robot," said the lion, looking over Harris's costume. "That's really cool! Maybe you'll actually win the contest instead of him!"

But not everyone was as impressed by Zeke's "costume."

A third-grader named Jeremy Jenkins walked up to Zeke and Harris in the hall. He wore a detailed monster costume, complete with fangs, claws, bulging eyes, and shiny, purple fur.

"These are the best costumes you guys could get?" Jeremy sneered. "They look cheap and homemade! My parents bought me this awesome monster costume. It was the most expensive one in the store."

Jeremy turned to Harris. "You look like a broken microwave," he said.

Then he pointed at Zeke. "Are you supposed to be an alien? You look like a giant green peanut. And those eyeballs are *soooo* fake!"

"*I've* got the best costume," Jeremy snarled. "And *I'm* going to win the contest!"

Harris saw Roxy looking at them from down the hall. She appeared concerned. But when she met eyes with Harris, she quickly turned around and walked away.

COSTUMES IN CLASS

6

GRACE HOPPER

HARRIS TOOK HIS SEAT IN MATH class. He found it hard to get comfortable with all the metal pipes on his arms and legs. He removed his helmet and tried to focus on the lesson.

Ms. Milton, the math teacher, walked into the room. She was wearing a kangaroo costume, complete with a long tail and a stuffed toy baby kangaroo bouncing up and down in her pouch. She looked out at her classroom full of wizards, monsters, and ghosts.

Zeke picked up a pencil with his tentacle and tried to write.

"What's the matter?" asked Dave Barrett. He sat next to Zeke and was dressed in a skeleton costume. "Don't aliens use pencils?"

Zeke said, knowing Dave wouldn't believe him, "Actually no, we don't. We usually use our minds to write things down."

Dave chuckled and all the bones on his costume shook.

Ms. Milton smiled. "Settle down, class. You all look wonderful!" she said. "But we still have to complete today's lesson."

Ms. Milton wrote a math problem on the board.

"Does anyone have the solution?" she asked.

69−27=

A girl dressed like a dolphin raised her flipper.

"Yes, Maria," Ms. Milton said.

"The answer is 42," Maria said, her dolphin mouth flapping open and shut as she spoke.

"Correct," said Ms. Milton. She turned to write the answer on the board, but her long kangaroo tail knocked a stack of books off her desk and onto the floor.

"I can see that it's just as hard being a kangaroo as it is being an alien!" she said, bending down to pick up the books as all the kids laughed.

At lunch, the cafeteria looked like the world's biggest costume party. Dinosaurs ate lunch next to witches, and a giant daffodil was seated next to a walking fish.

Harris took his usual seat next to Zeke. Zeke did his best to pick up a fork with a tentacle, but it slipped out before he could get some food on it.

"On Tragas, we use a long, thin utensil to eat with," Zeke whispered. "It easily rests on our tentacles. Or we can just levitate it up to our mouth, if we want."

Roxy walked over to their table. She was dressed in a sorceress costume, complete with a tall hat, a flowing orange and black gown, and a glowing magic orb. Her usual chair next to Harris and Zeke was empty, but Roxy kept on walking right past them to the opposite end of the table and took a seat there.

She must still be mad at me, Harris thought.

Zeke and Harris looked at each other. Harris decided to be brave and speak to her.

"Cool costume, Roxy," he said.

She turned away for a moment as if she didn't want to talk to Harris, but then turned back.

"Thanks," she said quietly.

Well, she spoke to me, Harris thought. *That's something.*

A few minutes later, Jeremy walked past their table carrying his lunch tray. He stumbled and his juice spilled all over Zeke.

"Oops," he said. "So clumsy of me. It can be hard to navigate in this amazing costume."

Jeremy stared at Zeke, expecting to see Zeke's costume ruined by the juice. But instead, the juice was absorbed right into Zeke's real skin.

"What—what happened to the juice?!" Jeremy asked, surprised.

Harris looked at Zeke. How was he going to explain this?

"My costume is made of special waterproof material," Zeke said.

"Oh well, lucky you," said Jeremy, moving along to his table.

Roxy slid her lunch tray down and took her usual seat next to Harris.

"Did you see that?" she asked. "He spilled that juice all over Zeke's costume on purpose! He was trying to ruin it."

"It could have been an accident," Zeke said.

"Yeah, he probably just tripped," Harris added. Roxy seemed more mad at Jeremy than at him, which made Harris feel better.

"Well, I don't buy it," Roxy said, looking upset and almost scary in her sorceress costume. "I think he was trying to ruin Zeke's costume for the contest!"

7

RECESS

AT RECESS THAT AFTERNOON, a bunch of witches, goblins, and superheroes started a game of tetherball. Most of the kids had to take off parts of their costumes to be able to play. A pile of claws, capes, clown faces, and magic wands sat in a large pile on the side of the tetherball court.

Jeremy, with his monster head and claws off, called out to Zeke.

"Hey, Zeke!" he shouted. "Wanna play?"

"Sure," Zeke said. He floated over to the court.

"You probably have to take off your costume, right?" Jeremy asked.

Nearby, Roxy leaned over and whispered to Harris. "Jeremy wants Zeke to take off his costume. I bet he wants one of his friends to hide it or rip it or something when Zeke isn't looking!"

"I don't know," said Harris. "Everyone took off parts of their costumes."

"That's okay. I can play with my costume on," Zeke said.

"I think you'd do better with your costume off," Jeremy insisted. "Why don't you take it off? I just want it to be a fair game. Don't want to beat you too badly!"

"You see?" Roxy whispered on the sidelines.

"Hmm, Jeremy *is* being kind of pushy about it," Harris agreed.

"I'm fine like this," Zeke said. "Let's play."

Jeremy scowled, then started the game.

Using his tentacles to whack the ball again and again, Zeke easily won the game.

"I was just taking it easy on you," Jeremy said, then he snatched up the rest of his costume and stomped off.

On the way to his final class of the day before the contest, Harris stopped in the bathroom. He walked into a stall, closed the door, and heard some other kids come in. Although he couldn't see him, Harris clearly overheard Jeremy's voice.

"I can't let that new kid, Zeke, win the contest," Jeremy said. "My costume is still clearly much better, but I don't want to take any chances!"

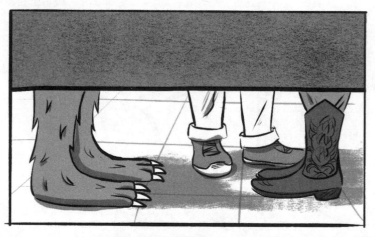

"So what are you going to do?" asked the kid Jeremy was talking to.

"I snuck a sack of flour out of the cafeteria," Jeremy said. "I'm going to use it to ruin Zeke's costume!"

"Good plan!" said the other kid, snickering.

Roxy was right about Jeremy! Harris thought. *I've got to warn Zeke!*

8 SABOTAGE!

ONCE HE HEARD JEREMY LEAVE, Harris rushed out of the bathroom to find Zeke. He ran down the hall, turned a corner, and ran right into Roxy.

"Careful! Where are you rushing to?" asked Roxy.

"You were right about Jeremy!"
Harris said urgently. "I just overheard
him talking in the bathroom. He plans
to ruin Zeke's costume by dumping
flour all over it!"

"That's terrible!" Roxy shouted. "We
have to find Zeke and warn him."

Harris and Roxy hurried through the school looking for Zeke. After searching the halls and classrooms, they finally spotted him at the far end of a hallway. He was about to go into the gym for his final class of the day. But before they could reach him, they saw Mr. Mulvaney, the gym teacher, come up behind Zeke.

"Let's go, son. You don't want to be late for class do you?" Mr. Mulvaney said to Zeke.

Zeke pulled open the gym door. He sensed something falling from above his head. Before he even knew what it was, Zeke used his powers to redirect it so it wouldn't hit him. He hoped that whatever it was would land harmlessly on the floor.

But instead, it fell right on top Mr. Mulvaney. A cloud of white exploded right on the gym teacher's head, and Zeke looked over to see him covered in flour. Some flour had also landed on Zeke.

Zeke spun around, sending his tentacles wrapping around his body. "Mr. Mulvaney! Are you all right?" he asked.

"Who would pull such a prank?!"
Mr. Mulvaney asked, brushing flour
angrily off his shoulder.

"I don't know," said Zeke. "It looks
like I got some on me, too."

"Don't worry, I'll get to the bottom
of this!" said Mr. Mulvaney. Then he
stormed off to clean himself up before
class.

Harris and Roxy, who had seen all of this, rushed up to Zeke. They quickly filled him in on Jeremy's plot to ruin his costume.

"Then that was meant for me!" Zeke said, realizing what had just happened.

"It sure looks that way," said Roxy. "Jeremy is trying to cheat to keep you from winning the contest."

"That makes me mad," said Zeke. "I really want to beat him now!"

"Looks like you got some flour on your costume," said Harris pointing to a few patches of white on Zeke's tentacles.

"I'll clean up after class," said Zeke, then he headed back into the gym.

"Did that bag seem to fall strangely to you?" Roxy asked Harris. "Like it almost changed direction in midair?"

"Uh . . . no!" Harris said nervously. "Let's, um, get to class!"

When classes ended, all the kids streamed toward the auditorium for the costume contest. Harris and Roxy arrived backstage along with the other contestants.

Harris smiled at the collection of costumed kids.

"Where's Zeke?" he asked Roxy, looking around for their friend.

"Maybe he's still in the bathroom cleaning off the flour," Roxy said.

"He's taking a really long time," said Harris, now getting a little worried. "I'm going to check on him."

Zeke stood in the bathroom, wiping the last of the flour off his tentacles and stomach.

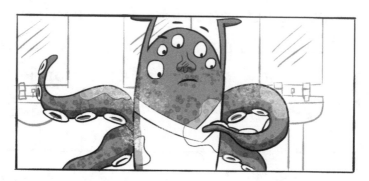

Once he was clean, he headed to the door. Wrapping a tentacle around the doorknob, he turned and pushed. The door didn't budge.

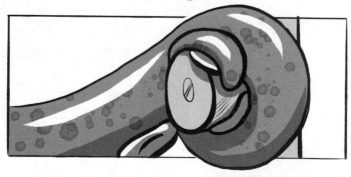

Hmm . . . that's strange, he thought. He pushed again, harder, but still the door wouldn't open. *Oh, no! I'm stuck in here! I'm going to miss the contest . . . and Jeremy is going to win!*

9 THE CONTEST

HARRIS RUSHED TO THE BATHROOM.
When he got there, he was stunned to see a chair propped up against the the door, wedged under the doorknob.

Harris pulled the chair away and flung the door open. He found Zeke inside, hovering back and forth nervously.

"Harris!" Zeke cried. "I couldn't open the door."

"That's because someone propped a chair up against it out here," Harris explained. "And I think we both know who did it."

"I can't understand why Jeremy would go to so much trouble to cheat just to win the contest," Zeke said. "I want to win, too, but cheating? What do you even get for winning?"

"The top three get a small medal, and the overall winner also gets a get-out-of-homework-free pass to use once."

"That's it?" Zeke asked. They both laughed.

"Well, there's bragging rights, too. We've got to stop him!" said Harris.

The two friends ran back to the auditorium, with Harris's robot legs clanking and Zeke's tentacles flapping.

Backstage, they caught up with Roxy and told her what Jeremy had done.

"We have to stop him before the contest starts!" said Roxy.

Harris, Zeke, and Roxy found Jeremy.

"You've been trying to ruin my costume all day! You tried to spill juice on it earlier," Zeke blurted out.

"And then you tried to drop flour on it. And you locked Zeke in the bathroom when your first plan failed," Harris added.

Jeremy pulled off the head of his monster costume and smiled.

"Who . . . me? You have no proof!" he said.

"Attention, contestants!" came an announcement over the backstage loudspeaker. "The contest is about to begin. Please come to the stage."

"Excuse me," said Jeremy, slipping his monster head back on. "I've got a contest to win!" Then he walked toward the stage.

"What are we going to do now?" asked Harris.

"I've got an idea to stop him," said Roxy. "Follow me."

Roxy, Harris, and Zeke ran onto the stage and over to the judges' table. The judges were teachers in the school, including Mr. Mulvaney.

"Jeremy Jenkins is a cheater!" Roxy said, pointing just offstage where Jeremy waited.

"What makes you say that, Roxy?" asked Ms. Milton, still in her kangaroo costume.

"He tried to ruin Zeke's costume by spilling juice on it," Roxy said.

"And he also tried to get Zeke to take his costume off during recess so he could steal and hide it," added Harris.

"And then he propped a sack of flour over a door so it would fall on me and ruin my costume," said Zeke.

"Well, it fell on me, instead," said Mr. Mulvaney, still obviously annoyed. "But how do you know that Jeremy did all those things?"

"I overheard him talking about his plan," Harris added.

"That's a lie!" said Jeremy, who came running out onto the stage.

"Really?" asked Mr. Mulvaney, getting up to take a closer look at Jeremy. "Then why do you have flour all over your shoulders? Zeke and I were the only people who got hit with it. But someone who lifted a sack over his head would most likely also have flour on him. . . ."

Jeremy looked down at his shoulders. He cringed at the sight of flour stuck to his purple fur.

"You, young man, are disqualified for cheating!" said Mr. Mulvaney. "You and your flour can go wait in the principal's office!"

Jeremy, still in his monster costume, hung his head and shuffled out of the auditorium.

The contest finally began. One by one, kids in their costumes paraded onto the stage and past the judges.

Roxy marched across the stage, her long gown flowing, her magic orb glowing. As each kid had their turn, the audience of students, teachers, and parents applauded. The judges scribbled notes about their costumes.

A gasp filled the auditorium as a huge dragon lumbered out onto the stage. It was eight feet long. Its tail waved back and forth. Streams of red ribbons flickered from the dragon's mouth, giving the look of flames coming from the fire-breathing beast.

It was the Reynolds twins, one wearing the dragon's head, the other its body. The audience applauded wildly. The judges scribbled furiously.

"Wow!" Harris whispered to his friends backstage. "That is a great costume. I guess we didn't see it before because they couldn't wear it at the same time in class!"

"You're next," Zeke whispered.

Harris clunked and clanked his way across the stage stiff-legged, with his antenna blinking brightly. Again, the audience applauded wildly and the judges made some notes.

Then it was Zeke's turn. He floated across the stage waving his tentacles in the air. His eyes bounced up and down, and he wiggled his antennae. Zeke got a nice round of applause, too.

When the last costumed student had crossed the stage, the judges gathered in a huddle. A few minutes later, they were ready to announce the winners.

Mr. Mulvaney stood up and spoke: "Third place goes to Zeke for his alien costume. Second place goes to Harris for his robot costume. And first place goes to the Reynolds twins for their amazing dragon costume!"

The audience gave another loud round of applause, and the winners were all given their medals.

"I DIDN'T WIN," ZEKE SAID, sounding surprised and a little disappointed.

"Sure you did," said Roxy. "Just because you didn't come in first doesn't mean you're not a winner."

"I'm happy," said Harris, pulling off his robot head. "I never won anything before. This is so cool!"

Roxy smiled.

"And Roxy," Harris continued. "I promise, next year, the three of us will make our costumes together."

"Yeah, and maybe next year, the three of us will win the top three spots!" said Roxy.

That night, the three friends, wearing the same costumes they wore to the contest, went out trick-or-treating together.

"Ooh," said one woman as she put candy into Zeke's bag. "That is a wonderful costume. Why, if I didn't know any better, I'd say you just landed here from another planet!"

"Thank you," said Zeke.

"I heard that Jeremy was grounded by his parents for that stunt with the flour," Harris said, as they moved onto the next house. "He's missing Halloween this year."

"It's funny, he was so concerned about Zeke's costume, but even Harris and the Reynolds twins beat Zeke!" Roxy said.

"Thanks for reminding me," Zeke said, and they all laughed.

At the next house, a man opened the door and said, "Nice costumes!" He turned to Zeke and asked, "What are you supposed to be?"

"I am supposed to be holding out my bag and getting candy from you," Zeke replied, straight-faced.

Harris and Roxy cracked up. Zeke didn't understand what was funny.

He still has a ways to go to understand humans! Harris thought.

"No, Zeke," said Roxy. "He means what is your costume."

"Oh," Zeke replied.

"He's an alien," Harris said.

Zeke smiled at Harris.

This is one time I can say that without giving away Zeke's secret, Harris thought. He could tell that Zeke was thinking the same thing.

Then the sorceress, the robot, and the alien, laughing and talking, moved on to the next house.

A. I. NEWTON always wanted to travel into space, visit another planet, and meet an alien. When that didn't work out, he decided to do the next best thing—write stories about aliens! The Alien Next Door series gives him a chance to imagine what it's like to hang out with an alien. And you can do the same—unless you're lucky enough to live next door to a real-life alien!

ANJAN SARKAR graduated from Manchester Metropolitan University with a degree in illustration. He worked as an illustrator and graphic designer before becoming a freelancer, where he now gets to work on all sorts of different illustration projects! He lives in Sheffield, UK.

anjansarkar.co.uk

LOOK FOR MORE BOOKS IN THE
ALIEN NEXT DOOR SERIES!

ELLA AND OWEN

Dragon twins Ella and Owen are always at odds. Owen loves to lounge and read, but adventurous Ella is always looking for excitement. Join these hilarious siblings as they encounter crazy wizards, stinky fish monsters, knights in shining armor, a pumpkin king, and more!

Tales of SASHA

Meet Sasha, one very special horse who discovers she can fly! With the help of her best friend, Wyatt, Sasha sets out to find other flying horses like her. Come along on their adventures as they explore new places and make new friends.

Isle of MISFITS

Gibbon is a gargoyle who doesn't like to sit still. But a chance meeting brings him to an island filled with other mythical creatures and a special school for misfits like him! Gibbon and his new friends get all the excitement they can handle in this magical series!

Mighty MEG

Meg's life is turned upside down when a magical ring gives her superpowers! But Meg isn't the only one who changes. Strange things start happening in her once-normal town. Can Meg master her new powers and find the courage to be the hero her town needs?